Anthology of Aussie romance stories

SPLASHES
of LOVE

FOREWORD BY JAN-ANDREW HENDERSON

Copyright ©2024 Splashes of Love

FIRST EDITION: 2024

978-0-9756535-0-0 (pbk)
978-0-6456589-9-6 (ebk)

The moral right of the author has been asserted.
Foreword © Jan-Andrew Hendeson
Meeting in a Maze © Anna Campbell
Contract of Love © A.K. Leigh
The March of the Eligible Bachelorettes © Jan-Andrew Henderson
Happy Endings © Charmaine Clancy
Brewing Love © Chris Radge
My Birthday Kiss © Lizz Curry
To Take a Lover © Kellie M Cox
A Good Man © Christine Betts
Old Long Since © Selena Jane
Kickstart my Heart © Debbie Kahl
Lost. And Found © Angela Victor
The Desert Flame © Jared Krantz
Plus One © Martin Clancy
Thirty-eight Degrees South © Jodi Cleghorn

Rainforest Writing Retreat is not responsible for author websites or author social media (or their content) that are not owned by Rainforest Writing Retreat.

Cover layout by Charmaine Clancy
Lead editor and interior layout by Christine Titheradge
Interior edit by Gina Pinto
Interior support by Self-Publishing Lab

OTHER BOOKS

CONTENTS

FOREWORD

It's funny the things you learn at the Rainforest Writers Retreat. This year, one of the presenters told us romance was the oldest genre in the world, as well as being the most popular. That's a pretty powerful combination and it got me thinking. So, of course, I googled it.

Turns out, the genre is older than the word itself. Romance stems from the Latin term Romanicus—meaning simply 'speaking in the style of Rome'. This then became the basis for Romance languages like French, Spanish and Italian, which is a pretty promising start.

The term then crops up in medieval France. Though there's often a damsel in distress lurking somewhere, it is mainly used to described tales of hunky heroism. By the 17th century it has been translated into English, changing to mean stories which feature imagination and inventiveness.

Truth is that the word has morphed more than the genre itself. I mean, what is a romance story anyway? Two people meet. They fall for each other. Something gets in their way. They overcome it. Fairly standard stuff, yet that template has lasted, virtually unchanged, for millennia.

Of course it has—and quite rightly so. It is more heroic to battle for love than out of hate or duty. The prize to be won is greater than riches or fame. And there's always a happy ending.

Nor is that outline particularly restrictive. With enough imagination and inventiveness in your storytelling you can transform it into something fresh and vibrant every time, ensuring the world's oldest story never gets old. In this case, there's the added themes of sun, sea and sand to guarantee a collection of stories you'll have a wonderful time reading.

Welcome to *Splashes of Love*.

—Jan-Andrew Henderson

MEETING IN A MAZE

anna campbell

Lapstone Court, Leicestershire, October 1815

'Oh.'

At the unexpected sound, Henry Melway glanced up from his sketchbook where he was trying—and failing—to capture the details of the marble fountain in front of him.

It was surprising the amount of displeasure one short syllable could convey. A displeasure mirrored in the expression of the girl glowering at him from the gap between two high yew hedges.

He'd been alone in the centre of Lord Furneaux's maze all afternoon. He'd assumed he'd stay that way. But he wasn't a barbarian. He had some manners. And anyway, the sketch really wasn't progressing.

1

He set his drawing aside and rose from the wooden bench. 'Lady Charlotte.'

The girl bobbed into a brief curtsy, although her scowl didn't lighten. 'Lord Eltham, I didn't mean to intrude.'

He tried the smile that had got him his way with the female half of the population since he was in his cradle seventeen years ago. 'I'd appreciate some company.'

The smile failed to work its usual magic. Charlotte Moore continued to regard him as if he was a slug in her salad.

She was an unusual-looking girl. Henry had already noticed her among the crowd of pretty, conventional poppets who proliferated at this house party in the flat Leicestershire countryside. He guessed that she must be about fifteen. His host, Lord Furneaux, had a couple of daughters around that age. Little blonde dolls Henry hadn't paid much attention to. They giggled.

All the girls in this house giggled.

All the girls. Except for this one, with her angular features, haughty nose, and emphatic dark brows. They were striking attributes, but they dominated what was still essentially a child's face.

'No, I should go.' Her expression remained wary. 'I wanted—'

'A break away from the cats?'

She paused in turning to retreat through the maze behind her and cast him a puzzled glance. 'Do you mean the other girls?'

'I do.'

He had two older sisters, although they'd mercifully grown out of the spiteful stage. More, he'd noticed that this girl had been on the outer since she'd arrived. In fact, he was surprised quite how much he'd noticed.

He even noticed that the girl's abundant black eyelashes were wet and clumped. Somewhere recently she'd indulged in a bout of furious tears.

The wariness became more marked when she surveyed him as if unsure whether he meant to bite her. 'What do you care? Everybody likes you.'

The resentful remark betrayed her unspoken fear that nobody liked her. 'Of course they do. I'm the heir to an earldom. They're currying favour.'

With a shake of her head, she took a hesitant step towards him. She wore a crumpled muslin gown in a bilious shade of yellow that made her translucent skin look muddy. Whoever was in charge of dressing her should be shot.

'No, that's not it. People like you for yourself. The boys want to be your friend and the girls want you to pay them attention.'

It seemed she'd been watching him, too. How... *interesting*.

'You're very kind.'

Her lips turned down at his response. 'No, I'm not. I'm very envious. Nobody wants to talk to me.'

He tried a smile again, and this time he caught a glimmer of softening. 'That's not true. I do.'

When she rolled her eyes, he laughed. Most of the girls he knew were too busy trying to look pretty to risk making faces.

'How can I doubt it?' She ventured another step closer. 'That's why you're hiding here in the middle of Lord Furneaux's maze. Just in case I should wander along to entertain you.'

He sat down again, liking her wry humour. 'I admit I did skive off for a bit of privacy, but now you're here, I welcome the interruption. Won't you come and join me?'

Henry expected her to demur, or even take to her heels. She was shyer than the other girls, too, which didn't help her to fit in. He wasn't by nature given to poetic flights, but something about this slender, dark-haired girl made him think of wild woodland creatures prone to disappear into the shadows at the first sudden movement.

'Now it's you being kind.'

He shrugged. 'Solitude was more appealing in my imagination than in reality.'

She cast him a searching look, then to his satisfaction, she perched on the edge of the bench about a foot away from him.

'Did you have trouble with the maze?' he asked when she didn't do anything to further the conversation.

'I got lost a couple of times. I came in here to escape Mary and Polly.'

The two meanest girls. And the pushiest. 'Me, too.'

When that roused a faint huff of amusement, he felt like he'd won a great victory.

'They do nothing except talk about you. Well, other than tell me I'm too ugly to live.'

Little witches. He'd like to wring their scrawny necks. 'I'm sorry.'

Her direct gaze startled him. With her colouring, he'd assumed her eyes would be brown, but they were a silvery grey of such clarity that he found himself staring back transfixed.

'It's not your fault.'

'I'm still sorry.' His smile faded, and he studied her with the eye of the artist he was at heart. When he spoke, his voice was slow and thoughtful. 'You know, I think you promise to blossom into a very interesting woman.'

'That's nice of you.'

He gave a short laugh. 'You sound surprised.'

'I just ... I just never thought you'd bother talking to me.' She went back to avoiding his stare, and nervous fingers began to pleat the skirt of the frightful frock. 'After all, you're so popular and clever. And handsome. Like a Greek god.'

'Why, thank you.' To his chagrin, he felt himself redden. Although not as violently as Lady Charlotte blushed. Her cheeks were as scarlet as ripe strawberries.

'I do beg your pardon.'

She cast him a quick sideways glance under those sumptuous lashes. She didn't intend flirtation, but nevertheless, his heart slammed to a stop. One day, she'd do that to lure a lover, and the lucky fellow's world would turn upside down.

He cleared his throat. 'For giving me such an extravagant compliment? I'm appalled. You should be hounded from good society, my girl.'

Her gurgle of laughter pleased him. He'd hated to think of her crying her eyes out over nasty nonsense. 'I think good society has decided I'm not fit to be seen anyway.'

Henry's lips tightened with annoyance. 'You shouldn't listen to those flibbertigibbets. You just haven't grown into yourself yet. When you do, all those silly little girls will look as boring

5

as white paint. Whereas you're going to blossom into someone unforgettable.'

Ever since she'd spouted that drivel about Lord Eltham looking like a Greek god, Charlotte had been writhing with embarrassment. But this praise was astonishing enough to banish her mortification.

She gaped at him. 'Un ... unforgettable?'

His smile was kind. And sincere. She told herself that she shouldn't believe him, but he looked as if he meant what he said. 'Yes. And irresistible. Even now, you stand out from the crowd as special. That's why the other girls are picking on you. They're jealous.'

'I'm ... speechless.'

Actually she was flabbergasted. She'd never pictured herself speaking a single word to the universally admired Lord Eltham. She'd never pictured Lord Eltham paying her enough attention to give her the opportunity to speak that single word to him.

But here she was in his company, and he was saying all sorts of marvellous things. The sort of marvellous things that she'd never imagined anyone saying to her at any time. Let alone the handsomest young man she'd ever seen.

It was no wonder that all the girls sighed over him. Even Charlotte had devoted a few useless daydreams to the tall young viscount with his golden hair and golden skin.

Except it seemed that those daydreams hadn't been anywhere near as futile as she'd assumed. She wanted to pinch herself, but she'd already been gauche enough for one afternoon, thank you very much.

Half-convinced of his candour, she studied his face for any sign that he mocked her. But the dark blue eyes in those chiselled features remained steady.

'In fact, I'd like to draw you, if you'll allow me.'

'But aren't you drawing something else?'

She liked the hint of self-deprecation in his laugh. As if she didn't already like everything about him.

Apart from the fact that despite his kindness this afternoon, he would always be out of her reach. He might say nice things to cheer her up. But when their minds turned to romance, young bucks like Viscount Eltham sought out diamonds of the first water, not odd-looking misfits like Charlotte Moore. However interesting he might deign to call her.

'I was making a dog's dinner of trying to catch this blasted fountain. I'm much better with portraits. Do say you'll let me sketch you.' His voice lowered into seriousness. 'I'd like to show you what I see when I look at you.'

If anyone had asked Charlotte an hour ago if she'd agree to someone poring over her much-maligned features, she'd have shrieked in horror. But something inside her had changed since she'd blundered her way into Lord Furneaux's maze.

When she turned towards Eltham, she even managed to sound composed. 'I'd be happy to sit for you.'

She'd seen that brilliant smile often since she'd arrived at this purgatory of a house party a week ago. But up close, the flash of straight white teeth and the flare of pleasure in those impossibly blue eyes had a devastating effect on her efforts to behave like a well-brought-up young lady. Instead of an over-emotional idiot.

'Capital.' He rose and crossed to sit on the grass near the entrance to the clearing. With an eagerness that she couldn't help but find flattering, he turned to a fresh page of his sketchbook. 'Just look straight at me.'

'Should I smile?'

'No. It's too hard to hold a smile.' Already he danced his pencil over the paper with a speed that bewildered her.

Over the next half hour, they barely spoke. Whenever he paused in his drawing, Eltham examined her with a concentrated attention that nobody had devoted to her before.

Her eccentric father loved her, she knew, but he was more interested in her intellectual development than in what he viewed as frivolous worldly matters like her appearance. Her governess, Miss Peters, only looked at her to nag about some failing.

This probing, unflinching, but essentially benevolent gaze was unfamiliar. For the first time in her life, she felt accepted, not judged wanting. It was a powerful sensation, and one she promised herself she wouldn't forget.

When Eltham was in company, his quicksilver expressions gave an impression of endless vitality. But during this quiet interval, Charlotte had a chance to see past the surface glitter to the warmth and intelligence beneath.

She suspected that Eltham would remain a handsome man into old age. Perhaps even more handsome than he was now, once the character and humour he'd demonstrated today had a chance to mark his features.

At last, his busy pencil stilled, and he glanced up at her with a smile in his eyes, but not on his lips. 'I think that's the best I'm going to do.'

Charlotte had relaxed to a point where she smiled back with an ease that she hadn't felt since she'd arrived at Lapstone Court. 'May I see?'

With a grace that made her foolish heart stutter, he rose to his feet and crossed the lawn to sit beside her. 'Of course.'

Only then did fear kick in. Fear that perhaps he might mock her after all. Fear that even if he didn't, the portrait might expose her as ugly and unlovable, just as those odious girls said she was.

With an unsteady hand, she accepted the sketchbook. For a moment, she was too afraid to look at the drawing.

'What do you think?' he asked.

To her surprise, the question held a hint of uncertainty. A useful reminder that the young viscount was as human as she was.

Or almost.

She made herself glance down at the picture. Her breath escaped in a gasp. 'It's ... lovely.'

A faint sound of amusement escaped him. 'You're lovely.'

Charlotte, trained to seek the truth in all matters, knew she should argue with that erroneous conclusion. But the face depicted was indeed lovely. Yet still unmistakably Charlotte Moore. She took in the drawing as a whole, struggling to work out how he'd managed to make the image both her and not her.

'Thank you.'

He laughed again. 'You sound so suspicious. I promise this is what you look like to me. When in a few years you have society at your feet, I hope you'll recall my prediction.'

The unlikelihood of that event occurring brought Charlotte back to reality with a bump that felt like relief. For a second there, the world had made no sense and the ground had shifted under her feet in a most unsettling fashion.

'I promise that should such a thing ever happen, I'll think of you.'

'Thank you,' he said without a hint of irony, which she appreciated.

She had a sinking feeling that she'd think of him anyway. Not just because he remained the most spectacular creature she'd ever beheld. Closer contact had only deepened her partiality. Something powerful inside her wished to heaven that the words he'd spoken today were true and that he'd leave this secret place inside Lord Furneaux's maze as changed as she would.

But she was no fool. Popular young men, however amiable they might be, didn't tumble headlong in love with skinny, clumsy fifteen-year-old girls in the space of an hour.

'May I keep the drawing?' he asked.

It would have been nice to have the portrait, but if Miss Peters found it—Miss Peters had an unpleasant habit of snooping—there would be too many intrusive questions. Charlotte closed the sketchbook and passed it back. 'If you like.'

He accepted the sketchbook and gave her another of those devastating smiles that made her asinine heart perform acrobatics. 'Thank you.'

She rose to her feet, regretting the way that real life started to impinge on this enchanted interval. 'I should go.'

She'd been alone with the viscount too long for propriety. At a house party, society's strict rules relaxed a little and she wasn't yet out of the schoolroom, but nonetheless this meeting developed the air of a tryst.

If only that were true.

Showing more of those perfect manners, Eltham stood, too. He bowed his gilded head. 'It's been a pleasure.'

With a shy smile, Charlotte dipped into a curtsy. 'Good afternoon, my lord.'

She turned onto the path that she'd followed to reach the centre of the maze. Could one's life transform in the space of an afternoon? She feared it could. But something told her that the silly girls at this gathering would never again make her cry.

Dempster House, Lorimer Square, London, May 1821

'By gum, the Incomparable's here. Prepare to be bowled over, old man. She makes every other debutante this year look as dull as ditchwater.'

As they progressed through the blue-blooded crush filling the Duchess of Granville's ballroom, Henry hardly listened to his friend. Ivor Bilson was always wittering on about something or other. Usually hunting and fishing. Although this time round, some female seemed to occupy the fellow's mind.

Henry was just back from his grand tour through Italy and France. While he did his best to hide it, he was still trying to

11

find his feet in London. He hadn't yet had a chance to assess the season's crop of marriageable misses.

A quadrille was ending. As he surveyed the crowded room, his attention snagged on a tall, dark-haired woman wearing white.

'Who is that?' he asked Ivor, as his heart began to race with excitement.

'Where?'

Not for the first time, Henry wished that his friend was quicker on the uptake. 'The lady over there with ... ' He dredged up a name from his school days. '... Anthony Comerford. The lady in white.'

Ivor made a sound of complaint. 'They're all in bally white. They're debutantes, don't you know? Makes a chap think he's lost in a blasted snowstorm, what? You'll have to do better than that, if you want me to pick one filly out from the rest. Comerford, you say?' Then his tone changed. 'That's her.'

Henry had a powerful inkling that was indeed her. 'Who?'

'I told you. The incomparable Lady Charlotte Moore. She's taken the beau monde by storm. Rumour is half the single gentlemen in England have offered for her.'

'Has ... ' Henry's mouth turned as dry as a desert, making speech difficult. He'd come back home feeling that he could make some claim to Continental sophistication. Now one glimpse of a beautiful girl left him completely at sea. 'Has she accepted any of them?'

'No. Not yet.'

Henry smiled at his friend. 'Ivor, you're the herald of joy.'

Confusion clouded Ivor's good-natured features. 'Herald of ...

Henry didn't linger to explain. Instead he strode across to where the Incomparable stood in a group of people, idly fanning herself.

'Lady Charlotte, I believe this is my dance.' He was in such a state, he only just remembered to bow.

She turned in surprise. As those extraordinary silver eyes settled on him—they'd been extraordinary even in the unformed young girl he'd met all those years ago—he prayed that she remembered him.

'Lord Eltham.' She performed a curtsy considerably more assured than her adolescent effort. That sunny afternoon at Lord Furneaux's estate, she'd been all coltish awkwardness. But even then, Henry had known that she'd become remarkable.

Clearly the rest of the world had come around to that opinion.

'Dash it, Eltham,' Comerford protested, as the orchestra played the introduction to the next dance. To Henry's pleasure, a waltz. He very much liked the prospect of holding her in his arms and not having to change partners. 'Lady Charlotte's promised to dance with me next.'

'I asked quite a while ago.' Henry didn't look away from grey eyes that expressed curiosity and what he hoped was pleasure at their reunion. 'Perhaps the lady has forgotten?'

Unlike Ivor, Lady Charlotte had a brainbox in tiptop working order. Her lush pink lips curved in a smile that made Henry's breath catch. By God, she was a beauty.

'I haven't forgotten.' Something restless and troubled inside Henry settled as she turned to Comerford, that glorious smile taking on a hint of apology. 'I fear, my lord, that you may have to yield to the prior claim.'

Without giving Comerford another chance to object, Henry caught her arm. Even through his glove, the touch sent a surge of heat rushing through his veins. 'Shall we?'

'I'd be delighted.'

He hoped his smile wasn't too wolfish, although he wouldn't wager money on it. How wonderful that she wasn't coy. She'd been refreshingly genuine at Lapstone, he recalled. He was grateful that society's acclaim hadn't spoiled that.

He took her into his arms for the waltz. Such a simple action, yet all the same, his world reeled. Did she catch her breath at the contact, too? They began to move as if they'd danced a thousand times before.

'I've still got your portrait,' he murmured.

It was true. It was tucked into the back of his portfolio.

Life since he'd met Lady Charlotte Moore had been packed with excitement and experience, and he'd be lying if he said that he'd pined over the drawing. But every so often, he'd glanced at it with a vague feeling of unfinished business awaiting his attention.

'After all this time?' Her lips twitched with the humour that reminded him of the girl he'd met so long ago. He remained surprised how well he remembered every second of that encounter. 'Surely you've found better things to draw than over-emotional chits.'

'Charming young ladies.'

'That's a matter of opinion.'

'I'd welcome the opportunity to draw you again.'

She arched her eyebrows with a hint of elegant hauteur that stole his breath. What an alluring woman that interesting young girl had become. 'I'm under a little closer supervision in London than I was at Lapstone, my lord.'

'No convenient mazes to hand?'

The sound of her laugh made his heart lift. 'Unless we try the one at Hampton Court?'

His hold on her waist firmed and brought her nearer, within a whisker of impropriety. He wanted to kiss her. Hell, he wanted to steal her away and discover all her secrets. But this was Mayfair, and there were rules about how a man pursued a woman he wanted.

'Or perhaps we could choose a more conventional path, and I could call on you tomorrow?'

His heart expanded when a sparkling silver gaze rose to meet his. 'I'd like that.'

Henry reminded himself that he was in the middle of a ballroom in Lorimer Square. He couldn't whoop with triumph like a hobbledehoy because he'd obtained her agreement. Much as he might like to.

He restricted himself to a low purr of satisfaction. 'So would I, my dear Lady Charlotte. So would I.'

Happiness surged in his blood as he began to whirl Charlotte around until he felt like they were flying.

CONTRACT OF LOVE

a.k. leigh

'Hot customer wants to see you out front.'

From her desk, Chloe Talbot sent Adam, her best friend and assistant manager, a mock-reproachful look. 'That's inappropriate.'

'Sorry, Boss.'

The teasing tone told her he was not sorry and would do it again. *Lucky you love him.*

She aimed an unimpressed look his way, making him grin as she continued, 'What's his complaint?'

Complaints were the usual reason someone requested the owner-manager.

'Don't know, but he asked for you by name.'

She raised an eyebrow, intrigued. 'Did he give you his name?'

'No, and I forgot to ask.'

'Too dazzled by his looks?'

'You know me too well.'

She sighed. The unexpected interruptions that came with running a business could be frustrating. Whatever the problem, hopefully, it would be a quick fix that resulted in a satisfied customer.

As she stood, she said, 'This had better be worth it.'

'*He* is.' Adam grinned.

'You are terrible.'

'Guilty.'

She chuckled, then walked to Adam's side and peeked around the office door. A stranger stood towards the back of the store. The blue-black colour of his hair reminded her of Superman. Even his stance hinted at her favourite superhero: side profile with one hand on his hip, while scanning the pages of an open book. When her attention came to his tanned, clean-shaven face, Chloe's skin rushed with a prickle of heat. Never had she been more grateful for the blasts of cool air coming from the roof ducts.

Adam gave a playful nudge to her side. 'Was I right, or was I right?'

'You were right.'

The man was *super* hot. She ogled the length of the stranger's body. An expensive-looking white business shirt and navy pinstriped pants hid his physique, which sent her brain into a frenzy of imaginings. He didn't appear beefy or untoned, but somewhere in the middle. *The way you like it*. Compared to him, her cheap denim shorts and simple capped sleeve shirt felt underdressed.

'Do you know him?'

'Nope.'

But wishing you did right now . . .

Adam sighed, 'It's a shame he's straight.'

'Why do you say that?'

'He didn't check me out.'

She play-smacked him on the arm. 'You have such an ego sometimes.'

'Guilty again.'

She shook her head, faux-mocking, as she smiled.

Adam's tone turned serious when he said, 'Then again, he asked for you by name, so maybe he saw you before he saw me. In which case, I stand no chance.'

'Aww. Now that's the sweet-talker I know and love.'

Adam wrapped one arm around her shoulder and pulled her close to him. 'I love you, too. Now, go out there and get his number, so at least one of us can have some fun tonight.'

He held up his fist; she obliged him by bumping it.

She took a step outside her office just as the shop's door opened. A tinkle from the bell above the door greeted a group of bikini-clad women who entered. The popularity of their Gold Coast town attracted an array of tourists and Aussies. Many of whom wanted something to read while they sunbathed.

Adam exited the office and said to the group, 'Welcome to *Talbots*. How can I help you?'

Chloe watched the Superman look-alike note the newcomers, before he swept his gaze around the store and stopped on her. He smiled and offered a single wave of recognition. He knew who she was. But she didn't recognise him. *No way you would forget someone who reminds you of Superman.*

The stranger turned to replace the book to the shelf. Chloe took that as her cue to approach. As she reached him, and opened her mouth to say something, the stranger turned around. Except, he mustn't have realised she'd been on her way to him because he took a wide step as he turned, and collided with her. The impact sent her reeling backwards into one of the keepsake tables dotted around the bookstore. A stinging sensation pulsed from her arm and made her hiss while she tried to right herself. She saw the stranger step forward. His hands, one on her back and the other on her forearm, distracted her from the stinging as he helped her straighten.

When he released his grip, he asked, 'Are you hurt?'

Unable to stop it, another hiss escaped her mouth. She pulled her left arm up to shield her injured right one in an instinctive cradling gesture. His sea-blue eyes stared into her brown ones, while his brow creased with visible concern. The Man-of-Steel features appeared even more stark up close. Her heart gave an odd little flutter at the realisation.

'You're bleeding. I need to put pressure on the wound. It might hurt.'

Before she could answer, he stepped closer, and an intoxicating scent of saltwater drifted from his skin. She could almost taste the salt on her tongue. *Must have been in the ocean this morning.* He pulled a white handkerchief from his shirt pocket and pressed it to the tender flesh of her biceps. Instead of the pain he'd prepared her for, a ripple of soothing warmth dulled the ache.

The stranger cut into her numbed bliss by calling out, 'Can I get some help here, please?'

Adam strolled around the corner of a bookshelf, as though unaware of the chaos that had unfolded; he'd probably been flirting with a customer. He bolted to her side once he saw the injury.

Clear distress crinkled the corners of his mouth. 'What happened?'

'Some loose metal siding on the table sliced her arm. Can you get the first-aid kit?'

Adam rushed off as she glanced down to inspect the damage. A wave of light-headedness flowed over her with the movement.

'Whoa. Let's get you seated.'

The stranger placed his arm around her back, then guided her onto the wooden bench close to her office door. He sat beside her. The size of the bench forced their closeness. He gave her a reassuring smile while keeping pressure on her wound. When she winced, he thumbed light strokes over her unwounded skin. The simple action wrapped her in soothing comfort, like honey in lemon tea.

While they waited for Adam, she studied the stranger's hands. They looked like surfers' hands—strong and sea-tamed ... and covered with splotches of her blood. She tried to pull away.

He held fast. 'You're still bleeding.'

'Yes, all over you.'

He shrugged. 'Seems fair. I caused the injury.'

The word 'injury' sent an unpleasant conclusion shuddering through her. She'd have to email an incident report to the silent

21

partner who'd bought into her business and saved her shop from closure during the pandemic. How would he react? Whenever she emailed him with something unexpected, he responded in different ways. Yet, he insisted on instant compliance with his sporadic ideas, like having 'rustic' keepsake tables spread around the bookstore.

Adam returned with the first-aid kit and handed it to the stranger.

To her, Adam asked, 'Are you all right?'

'I'll live.'

The stranger rifled through the first-aid kit. Pulling out several items, he attended to her wound with practised movements.

'You've done this before?'

He nodded. 'I'm a volunteer part-time lifeguard.'

Ah. They learnt first-aid. Also explained the tan, saltwater scent, and surfer vibes despite the business attire.

The stranger dabbed at her wound with an ointment he'd taken from the kit.

'Ouch.'

'Sorry. I'll try to be more gentle.'

The warm tone and caring look he aimed at her made her grateful to be seated.

Adam cleared his throat. 'Guess you don't need me anymore.'

The teasing tone jolted Chloe's attention from the stranger.

She peered up at her friend. 'Thank you, Adam.'

'No problem.'

He went to walk away, but she stopped him when a thought came. 'Can you pick up anything that fell? The last thing we need is someone else hurting themselves.'

'Ugh. Can you imagine *his* reaction if that happened?'

'Yes, which is why I want to avoid it. It's already going to be a nightmare to explain this.'

'It was an accident. I'm sure this lovely customer can vouch for you.' Adam tapped the stranger on the shoulder, then left to carry out his task.

The stranger glanced over at her. 'Who do you want me to talk to?'

She groaned. 'My silent business partner might have some questions for you. I'm so sorry.'

He shook his head. 'That won't be a problem because I––'

She cut him off, 'You say that now, but you don't know him. He can be a real grouch.'

The stranger cocked his head to the side in an interested gesture. 'How so?'

'He doesn't like surprises, and, in business, you can't plan for the unexpected.'

'Like being cut by loose metal on a table?'

'Exactly.'

The stranger nodded. 'You're all bandaged up.'

'Really?' She peered down. 'You did a great job.'

'Thank you. It's common feedback. That, and being a grouch who doesn't like surprises.'

His half-grin made her stomach sink.

Oh-oh.

23

'Are you—'

'Jesse O'Brien. Co-owner of *Talbots*.'

Crap. Her silent *billionaire* partner in the flesh. Not only had she, and Adam, insulted him to his face, but she'd also bled all over him. *Oh, God*. The handkerchief! Was it one of those fancy expensive ones?

Panic must have shown on her face because he said, 'Relax. I'm not here to lecture you.'

'You're not?'

'No.'

Confusion flooded her mind. In the two years he'd been her partner, they'd communicated solely by text and email. Messages that had often come across as blunt and demanding. Yet, the man seated beside her had shown himself to be caring, patient, and good-humoured. What was going on? She needed answers, and a cure for the knots tying themselves up in her stomach.

'Why *are* you here?'

'I'll explain, but first I want to make sure you're okay. Let me help you stand.' He reached around her waist and supported her while they stood up together. 'You've got more colour in your cheeks. How do you feel?'

Aside from the non-summer induced heat rushing over her from his body contact?

'Fine.'

'Any dizziness?'

'No.'

'Nausea?'

'Nope.'

Her heart, on the other hand, flapped around her chest like leaves in a windstorm. *I've got it bad.* For a man who confused her with contradictions. A man who was her *business partner.* She forced her heart to settle. It was insane to let silly reactions interfere with her business. A business she had fought to keep afloat. She had to remember her priorities.

'In that case, do you feel up for a business meeting now? If not, I'm happy to reschedule.'

'Funny, I don't remember you scheduling this one.'

He hesitated, as if considering her words. 'I can see that was inappropriate. I apologise. Can I email the details to you instead?'

What details? Whatever the reason for this unscheduled meeting, if it was bad, it was better to know sooner rather than later.

'It's fine. Let's have the meeting.'

Seated on opposite sides of her desk, Chloe mentally prepared herself for whatever Jesse had in mind. *What will it be this time?*

Jesse opened his mouth to speak, but Adam chose that moment to pop into the office and say, 'I've cleared everything up. How are you?'

'Good.'

'Do you need anything?'

'No. Yes. Can you handle the store by yourself for a bit? We're having a business meeting.'

'All right ...' Adam threw them both an interested glance before walking out and closing the door behind him.

'He cares about you.'

'Adam?'

'Yes.'

'I care about him, too.'

The remark earned a subtle eyebrow raise from Jesse. *Hmm.* What did that mean?

'I've bought the art gallery next door.'

Okay. Sudden change of subject and minimal small talk. This was more like the Jesse she knew.

'What's that got to do with me?'

His answer threw her even more off balance than he already had. 'I want to knock down the connecting wall to expand the bookstore. I want to add a sitting area and workshop area. You can host art appreciation nights, painting workshops, author readings, poetry slams—'

She held up her hands. 'Wait. You want to knock down the bookstore?'

'No. I want to renovate the bookstore.'

'During summer. Our busiest season.'

'I've got contractors. The work will take two weeks over—'

'We would lose customers. What about our reputation? The reviews? The money?'

'I can—'

'This is my only source of income, and the most important thing I have in my life.' She cringed at how pathetic that sounded out loud, but continued, 'I've already compromised with you so many times to keep this place running.'

Her chest heaved, fuelling the frustration, fear, and anger duelling for supremacy in her heart. How could she have been so foolish to believe she was attracted to this imbecile? Superman?

More like *Super Jerk*. Silence stretched out, thickening the air between them.

In a low voice, Jesse said, 'I've made a mistake, and it's upset you?'

Why did he sound uncertain? Wasn't it obvious?

'Of course!'

He frowned. 'I'm sorry. Verbal communication can be tricky for me. I assumed you knew you could veto everything I suggested.'

'Well, clearly, I didn't.'

He nodded. 'I should have double-checked. Sorry, Chloe.'

He *said what*? An actual *apology*. Not one of those half-assed 'I'm sorry you're upset' ones, either. The fiery anger from seconds earlier cooled.

He continued, 'You have my word that I won't go ahead unless you agree. How about I leave the proposal with you to read?'

Why would she want to read the proposal? From what he'd said, it sounded like the downfall of everything she'd worked so hard for.

He reached for an envelope half-sticking out of his pants pocket, placed it on her desk, and rose from his chair.

'You have my number. Let me know what you think.' He hesitated a moment, then added, 'Remember to replace your wound coverings every day until it heals.'

With that advice, he left her stunned. How could a man be both polite *and* infuriating?

Adam entered the office. Crinkles to the corners of his eyes showed his concern when he said, 'I heard yelling. What happened?'

'*This.*'

She picked up the envelope with her unwounded arm and flung it across the desk towards him. He picked it up, took the seat Jesse had vacated, then removed the paper from inside the envelope. As he flicked through, reading, her thoughts raced. *How dare Jesse come,* unannounced, *and make more demands.* Hadn't *he done enough?* She glanced at her bandaged arm and glared.

'Hang on, that was *Jesse O'Brien?*'

'Uh-huh.'

'Are we in trouble?'

'Not the kind you're thinking.'

'That's a relief.' He returned to reading. After several minutes, he looked up. 'Okay. What's the problem?'

What was up with all the men today, missing the obvious?

'He wants to tear down the store.'

'No. He wants to renovate it over two weeks, starting from Christmas Day.' *A time when most of the surrounding businesses closed, meaning limited impact on the store.* 'And turn it into a space that will attract tourists but also cater to the local creative community.'

'He didn't say that.'

Adam raised an eyebrow in his knowing-the-answer-already look, 'Did you give him the chance?'

Crap.

'Chloe, he even has a plan for the art gallery staff. He's going to pay them during the renovations, and hire them once we reopen, if you agree.'

'It says "if I agree"?'

'Yep. See.'

He showed her. Seeing the words on paper melted her residual iciness.

'He also has ideas that could bring in loads of new business. Art appreciation nights, painting workshops, author readings, poetry slams––' *Jesse said all this, but I didn't try to understand.* '––Writing classes, school holiday activities. He's thought this through.'

'I can see that now.' She bit her bottom lip, feeling contrite. 'I think I owe him an apology.'

'I bet.'

The long-term impact of Jesse's plan raced through her mind. Not only could it benefit the store, but it could be the best thing to happen to the community in years. Her heart thumped with bright visions of the future.

She picked up her phone and called Jesse's number.

He answered on the third ring. 'Should I take cover?'

At least he had a sense of humour.

'No. Can we talk? Properly this time.'

'Of course. I'm at the café around the corner, but I can come back to you.'

'It's all right. I'll come to you.'

The walk would give her time to rehearse an apology.

Hanging up, she said to Adam, 'I've got to meet him at the café. Can you hold the fort for a bit longer?'

'No problem.'

Five minutes later, she walked towards Jesse, seated in a private booth inside the café. When he spotted her, he stood, and she couldn't help noticing the spots of dried blood on his business shirt. *Ack.* He waited for her to sit before retaking his own seat. The display of manners sent a shot of appreciative warmth through her chest. *Remember, Jesse is your business partner. Don't let that reaction turn into anything more than appreciation.* She placed her handbag on the space to her right.

Before he had the chance to speak, she said, 'I'm sorry for my outburst. In case you can't tell, I'm passionate about the store.'

'Forget it. Besides, out of the two of us, I'd say causing the gash on your arm is worse than an impassioned rant. I'm just relieved you're okay and want to talk.'

'Me, too.'

'Can I order you a coffee?'

'I'll get too edgy if I have another one.'

'How about water?'

Now that he mentioned it, her throat was dry. 'Sure.'

She watched him pour water from the bottle on the table into a spare glass. He slid the filled glass towards her.

'Thank you.'

Their fingers touched as he let go of the glass, and she tried to ignore the tingle that snaked through her veins. He made eye contact as she lifted the glass to her mouth and sipped. The gesture felt intimate, as though she had accepted more than a drink of water from him. His mouth lifted at the edges, a sign of pleasure. Was he attracted to her as well? *You're being ridiculous.* He was sexy, somewhat mysterious, and she hadn't been laid in ages. Plus, he *had* reminded her of Superman. That was the only thing going on.

She lowered the glass at the same time as her gaze, then said, 'I came to give you this.'

Chloe reached into her handbag, grabbed the envelope she'd put inside, then handed it over. As soon as he touched it, she snatched her hand away to avoid more physical contact ... and knocked over the water bottle.

Jesse tried to grab it, but the bottle hit the table and splintered. 'Ow.'

'Are you okay?'

Jesse showed her his left hand. A slash of blood grew redder and thicker by the second across his palm. 'Got cut.'

No. She'd injured *him* now. Today was not going well.

Other customers turned in their direction.

The closest server darted to their table. 'Is everything all right?'

'Do you have a first-aid kit?'

A sense of déjà vu hit her with Jesse's question.

'Yes. I'll be back.'

While they waited, Chloe picked up a napkin and dipped it into her water glass. She used the makeshift cleansing wipe to blot the blood from Jesse's palm. He winced but made no complaint.

31

The server returned with a red container about the size of a musical jewellery box. Taking it, Chloe ignored the twinge of pain opening the lid caused to her own injury.

Jesse must have noticed her discomfort, because he said, 'I'll come closer.'

Using one hand, he scooted himself around the booth until their knees touched. A shock of electrical attraction passed through her, along with the memory of their earlier contact on the bench. She forced herself to ignore it. Now was not the time to indulge in silly emotions. In silence, she applied antiseptic cream and a dressing over his cut, then secured medical tape over the dressing to keep it in place.

A moment before she finished, he asked, 'Are you okay?'

'Shouldn't I be asking you that?'

'This is a minor cut. You have a gash.'

The server, who'd started cleaning their table, shot them an intrigued look, then carried on with their task.

'We can finish playing "yours is bigger than mine" now because I'm finished.'

He looked at the dressing, then teased her right back, 'You've done this before.'

She laughed and forced herself to let go of his hand. 'Once or twice.'

He picked up the envelope.

Chloe noted a splotch of blood smeared across the front as she said, 'Check the last page.'

He removed the papers and flicked to the end.

His eyes widened in disbelief when he looked back at her. 'You signed the agreement.'

'You didn't think I would?'

'Not in a million years.'

Couldn't blame him.

The server finished the clean-up and left them alone.

One corner of his mouth lifted before he said, 'This is my first ever blood contract.'

'Eww, can we not call it that?'

He showed her the front of the envelope. 'It's literally got blood on it.'

'I saw that before. Sorry.'

'So am I.' She sensed he referred to every misunderstanding that had passed between them over the two years he'd been her silent partner.

On that thought, something that had niggled at her tumbled out, 'Why haven't we talked face-to-face before now?'

He sighed. 'As I said, verbal communication can be tricky for me.'

'Why is that?'

He hesitated. 'Do you really want to know?'

'Of course.'

'I have hyperlexia, it's a neurodiverse condition.'

'Is it similar to dyslexia?'

'No, but you're not the first person to ask me that. Simplified, it means I'm better with written words than verbal communication.'

'Hence, the texts and emails.'

'Yes. But I still struggle with those sometimes, as you know.'

'I need to get more educated about neurodiversity.'

His eyes brightened, hinting that she'd touched some type of nerve, but in a positive way.

'What's that look for?'

'You're the first person who's ever said that to me.'

'About getting educated?'

'Mm-hmm. It's quite nice to hear.'

'I'm glad. Thanks for telling me.' He smiled, making her insides feel cosy. In the silence, something else occurred to her.

'I'm wondering how you knew what I look like?'

'The website.'

Ah. She'd forgotten her picture was on there.

'The photo didn't do you justice.' As soon as the words were out, he looked up at the café's ceiling in a recriminating action. 'Argh, I shouldn't have said that, should I?'

'It's okay. I liked it.'

He stared at her, his gaze relaxed ... and inviting. With the sound of the nearby ocean waves matching the rolling nerves in her stomach, the urge to plant her mouth against his overwhelmed her. He leant closer, making her breath hitch when the lingering saltwater scent of his skin filled her senses. *Mmm.* She would never tire of sea smell. *Especially coming from him.*

'Can I kiss you, Chloe?'

She nodded.

In a slow, agonising-wonderful movement, he slid closer and brought his wound-free palm to her cheek. She almost sighed into the tenderness of his touch. His gaze bore into her, asking for more than they could give in the middle of a café. She reached out and placed her good hand against his biceps.

Hmm. Bigger than he looks. That's promising ...

As a new round of heat washed through her body, Jesse leant forward and placed a soft, but lingering, kiss against her lips. She closed her eyes and let swirls of contentment mix with desire. When she thought she might implode from need, he pulled away. She opened her eyes, wanting to know why he'd stopped.

Before she could ask, he sandwiched her left hand between both of his and said, 'Will you come out with me tonight to celebrate our new venture?'

'I'd love that.'

Outside the restaurant later that night, Jesse smiled and opened his arms in a welcoming hug. Chloe stepped into his embrace as though they'd done it a million times before.

In her ear, he said, 'You look beautiful.'

The warmth of his breath trickled from her neck, down her spine, where it rekindled the desire he'd inspired at the café.

Somehow, she managed to say, 'So do you.'

'Should we head in?'

She nodded. He stepped back and crooked his arm towards her. She noticed he'd positioned himself on her uninjured side. *Considerate.* How had she ever thought otherwise? She accepted his outstretched arm and walked into the future with him.

SPLASHES OF LOVE

THE MARCH OF THE ELIGIBLE BACHELORETTES

jan-andrew henderson

History repeats itself only in that, from afar, we all seem to lead exactly the same life. We are all born; we all spend time here on earth; we all die. But up close, we have each walked down our own separate paths. We have stood at our own lonely crossroads. We have touched the lives of others at crucial points, for better or for worse. In the end, each of us has lived a unique life story, astounding and complicated, a story that could never be repeated.

Edward Bloor

'I wouldn't ask too much of her,' I ventured. 'You can't repeat the past.'

'Can't repeat the past?' he cried incredulously. 'Why of course you can!'

He looked around him wildly, as if the past were lurking here...

F Scott Fitzgerald. *The Great Gatsby*

Yesterfield. East Coast of Scotland. 2023

'It is autumn.

Swirls of yellow leaves dance in the grass hollows above the beach. They settle and rise with each gust of the biting wind, half-forgotten memories that will not stay buried. He kicks through one pile, enjoying the swish of his make-believe sacrilege. A cloud of bug-filled dust rises around him and he retreats to the play park, patting at his jeans as he sits on a swing. In the distance, a porcupine ridge of swaying masts and rigging announces the fishing fleet has returned to harbour—a reminder that not everyone sails for pleasure or to reach far-flung places.

The breeze picks up and chains creak softly around him. Even seats that are deserted join in. The roundabout is turning slowly as if he has just missed children at play. He lights a cigarette, shielding the flame with his hand.

Yesterfield 1981

Jenny
How's life? I'm in sec studies just now but all I do is sit and stare out the window. I fancy you like fuck. I wish you'd chuck Joanne so I can go out with you. Why should you like Joanne better? You never said you did anyway. I think about you most at school and at night times. I know I'm only sixteen, but I can still go out with boys that are nineteen.

I spend whole afternoons sitting with Frankie in Vissocchi's café under the shabby candy-striped awning. Neither of us ever say anything to each other so we must be comfortable with it. Or we couldn't strike up a proper conversation if our lives depended on it. I mean there's only the two of us. But he's always there and so am I.

We smoke John Player Specials, wear leather jackets and our earrings are in the left lobes. Frankie has streaked hair too but that's more a fashion mistake than a rebellious statement. The other customers stare at us disapprovingly.

'What?' I say, not looking them in the eye. 'Yobs will be yobs.'

Out the seccy hut window I can see the school playing fields. I can see an old woman walking along the sand with a wiggly bum. I can see the distant lighthouse. I can see too bloody much.

'Crash the ash, Mrs Smoker,' Frankie says. And he starts singing.
'Hello hello hello ... this is the lord God, can you hear? Hellfire and damnation's what I've got for you down here.'

For two minutes I can't stop thinking about you. I think I fell in love the minute I set eyes on you. Will you be in the Den when I get out at 4.00 pm? If you say no to going out with me, I'd still like to be your friend.

Crooky comes in.
'Fit like, wankers?'
'Hello, Mrs Smoker.'

Crooky flicks his fingers in front of Frankie's eyes to see if he's been taking magic mushrooms. In magic mushroom season, Frankie has a permanent crick in his back from walking bent over.

Joanne
Hey! When I asked what you and Frankie were doing crawling round Middlefield Park you told me you were looking for a contact lens.

Didn't know if you'd be shocked.

You remember when me and you went to Lucy's house to watch Salem's Lot on TV? Tracy and Jimmy Boyd got together and so did Lucy and Darren Ogden even though she's posh and he's fat. It was that kind of night. Lucy's parents were out, so after the film finished, she left the lights off. That was the first time you touched me properly. You put your hand up my jumper.

How could I forget?

I grabbed your wrist then I moved it somewhere more ... intimate. I couldn't see your face in the dark — but I'm pretty sure *it* was shocked.

Touché.

Yeah. You obviously didn't need to speak sexy and French to get what I wanted.

On the way home Joanne and I sit in the play park by the beach, with the stone train and the swings and roundabout. And the empty paddling pool. It's just as dark down here, though a thousand stars graffiti the night sky and gulls are screaming wraiths playing cosmic join the dots. Freezing too but that doesn't stop us. The thrill of being discovered is replaced by a more natural excitement. Besides, under that vast canopy — with the endless, timeless sea crashing over the shore — we feel too small for youthful indiscretions to matter. We talk for about two hours before I walk you home.

I didn't notice until bedtime that my tights now had seams up the front.

Why did the chicken cross the road?

Don't know.

To get its old age pension.

You get it?

'Yes ... hah, hah hah!' I tried to act cool like I was in on the joke. But you just looked puzzled.

The chicken didn't.

I kissed you goodnight and went in and made some toast. You don't like eating toast in my house because there's always

41

dog hair stuck to it. I looked out the window and could see the end of your cigarette glowing in the dark at the end of my street. It occurred to me that you were shortening your life so I knew where you were. But you probably just got cold.

She opens the back door to let her dog out and waves from inside the shaft of light.

My mum likes you. She thinks you have nice hair. I went to the Thistle Club last night but it was no fun without you. Frankie wants to get off with me but he isn't going to. And of course they played 'Ant Music'. I went to bed with the little stuffed panda you gave me.

I meet Joanne on the rebound from Emma. Emma chucked me for snogging Fiona Finlay. Fiona was Bill McCombie's girl, even though he was sneaking about with Carol Conner. Emma was sarcastic with a wonderful laugh and Psoriasis covered both ears until, eventually, they fell off. Well, her earrings did. Ripped right through the lobes, leaving two track marks like she was part of some exotic tribe. She wore scarlet straight-leg jeans over tights, white stilettos and her mother had an ashtray that belonged to Hitler. Or so she claimed. Emma got My Guy *and* Photo-Love *magazines delivered every week, so I'd come around on Saturday mornings and read them. Everyone thought she was hard as nails but she just had that kind of face.*

She was my first proper girlfriend and I was crazy about her.

Emma

You know one way or another you'll come back and get me. We'll end up together in ten years, cause you never forget your first love. I'll meet you in ten years.

I try to forget her by sitting on a summer seat. A magpie watching the schoolgirls flocking along the esplanade, catching their shiny precious glances. Girls that live in the country leave the car park on rust-flecked buses and can't come back at night to hang around the shorefront. Town girls are more sophisticated, anyway. Country girls seem bred to pull ploughs if their dad's tractor breaks down.

Short skirts have been banned by the headmaster, Mr Elder, so the girls have to establish their independence some other way. Buttons unfastened to the waist. Lipstick applied in the toilets and removed at garden gates. The March of the Eligible Bachelorettes, I call it. Surf crashes behind them and the sea glitters like a jewelled carpet—but they are louder and more eye-catching.

Job done.

I haven't seen you in ages. There's a song on the radio right now. I forget the band but the lyrics I think are about me and you.

'Coming home, through Jersey Heights

There's a dark red bedroom light

And he says, every bus ride

I've seen that window from the inside.'

43

I'm really sorry we split up now. I didn't realise how much I'd miss you. I enjoyed Friday. The Tannadice disco was great fun, probably because I was sloshed, pished and drunk.

Tannadice disco's where I first see Joanne. Then I meet her again at Northfield Youth Club when me and Frankie and Ed go up the youth club to play pool. Well, Ed goes to play pool. Me and Frankie go to check out the talent.

Hopefully I'll meet you on Monday. I hope you realise how much I love you. Please, please meet me on Monday behind the health centre after school and we can go sit on the swings and talk. If you can.

I fancy Tracy, really. Paul Morrison said he'd felt her tits in the school cloakroom and she hadn't even had them very long. Tracy is small, dark and sort of ... elfin. Joanne is small, blonde and sort of elfin too. In fact, Lucy is quite elfin as well. But she's tall and elves should have some sort of height limit.

Tracy plays four games of pool with me and I ask her out to the Kingoldrum disco. Well ... I ask if she's going and she says aye and she asks if I'm going, so I say aye as well. It's all in the ayes. Frankie says he would definitely stick it in her ear and shout sherbert.

The Kingoldrum disco is in a country hall with a mud paved drive out front and back road rutted by tractor tracks. Everyone makes their own way to it and back, which is the way with most things in life.

Hilly arrives on his yellow Kawasaki. Me and Ed try to hitch a lift from Yesterfield Boulevard. Lads are always cruising around there in grey Ford Cortinas, like sharks with acne, hoping to pick up someone who has missed the organised bus and doesn't look like the back of one. We have no luck.

The organised bus quickly turns into a mobile pub—a human Noah's ark with all the liquid inside. Girls share vodka and gin in paper cups. Paul Morrison manages to climb all the way into the luggage rack and sticks his tadger through the mesh.

Joanne

I came up on the Kingoldrum bus with Lucy and Gwen. We drank half bottle of vodka and a some unidentified liquid Lucy knicked from her parents booze cabinet. Peem Wilson's Vauxhall Viva got stuck behind us and we could see June in the passenger seat, like she always was, holding a can of Tennent's Super Lager. There was usually a green plastic strip with *Peem and June* written on it, stuck across the top of the windscreen. But Ed had unsuccessfully tried to rip it off for a laugh and now it just said '… m and June'

The crowd in the back seat started hugging each other, making kissy faces and chanting 'mmmm and June, mmmm and June.' Frankie flashed his arse at them and somebody stuck a cigarette in it.

Hey Joanne. You seen Tracy?

She couldn't make it. Emma isn't here either, in case you're wondering.

Really? Suppose I'll have to talk to you then, eh?

45

Suppose you will.

In the hall, I try to impress Joanne by making fun of my friends.
'That's Ed dancing over there.' Ed's corn-coloured hair flaps up
and down. 'The one that looks like he's trying to dislodge a parrot from
each shoulder without using his hands.'
Joanne giggles and I am encouraged.

'Who's that?'

'Eh? That's Frankie.'

'He looks like he's running on the spot.' I'd gotten the hang
of the game.

It's the 'I-have-just-seen-a-UFO school of boogie.' Frankie is lit
up by a disco ball right above. Because he's on mushies, it transfixes
him. I point to one head bobbing well above the rest. 'See the guy whose
dancing bears no resemblance to the music? That's Hilly.'
Joanne laughs again.

'Dancing bears,' I said. 'It would make a good name for a
band.'
At the end of the night came the slow songs. I was never able
to remember the first one we danced to. Might have been 'Baby,
I Love You' by the Ramones ...

Joanne gets back on the bus when the hall empties and Frankie climbs on the back of Hilly's bike for a dice with death. I leave the hall with Ed and we walk down the black leafy tunnel, away from Kingoldrum's lights. We know someone will pick us up. That's the whole point of the Kingoldrum disco. Picking people up.

'I thought you liked Tracy.' Ed kicks a can down the road. 'But it looks like you scored with Joanne. Yum, yum.'

'Yup. At least I got my elf.'

'What?'

'You don't get it?'

Ed doesn't get it.

Emma

I couldn't make it to Kingoldrum cause I was grounded by my parents. Mr Elder was walking along the esplanade, saw me smoking and told me to put it out.

'What time is it?' I asked.

'Four-thirty.'

'What time does school finish?'

'Four o'clock.'

'Then fuck off.'

Frankie and I sit in Vissocchi's. Crooky has gone home to watch Danger Mouse. I could go home too but the one day I do a flying saucer will land in the town square. Frankie starts singing.

'Flying saucer attack. I'm never coming back. Oh, oh, oh, once till it's over.'

Monday afternoon. grey skies. Half day. Everything closed.

47

Jenny

I go through the Den on my way home from school. That way, if I meet you, Joanne won't be able to see us. Nobody will. It's quiet here and the air is filled with insects.

The Den is a small green valley in a small seaside town and the Sunday school picnic was invented to fill it.

But most days you're in Vissocchi's when the school comes out.

The monument on the esplanade looks like some grimy workman's finger. It annoys the clouds. You can't see the town clock from the back of Vissocchi's but that's okay, cause it doesn't work. You can tell when it's 4.00 because a herd of schoolgirls start to pass the window and some drift through the door. Bridget Vissocchi shuffles past. A long striped apron swathes her body but we know by the way she walks that she has no legs. Just really long hips that extend right down to her feet. Or castors, like a well upholstered couch.

'Getta you feet down offa da seat!'

What, Eh? Frankie? What did she say?

Emma

It's ten past four. Maybe you couldn't make it. Maybe I was inside the health centre when you came past. I suppose I can give it a few more minutes.

Frankie slams his feet down but misses all three of Bridget's Pomeranians because they're smarter than him. Poor Bridget. Her prices are too high but it doesn't matter. Nobody ever buys anything. Crooky can make one hot Ribena last five hours.

'Goodbye Mrs Smoker,' Frankie says.

Bridget grunts and waddles into the back.

Joanne

I won't be able to see you in Vissocchi's at four today. Now that I know I got into Stirling Uni, I have to talk to my mum and dad about grants and stuff.

No sign of Joanne. But in come the schoolgirls, startling the door chimes. Bridget still hasn't noticed the Tampon Bunch hung up there yesterday. In comes Young Div and Young Doob and Helen with the mole, and wee Alison who doesn't love me anymore. In comes Fraz's girlfriend, Shirley with the big passionate head. In comes Jingles with the bells on her fringed white boots. The Young Mental Shade pile in and climb over the front seats, like stormtroopers into a tank. Frankie throws matches at them.

No Joanne.

Right. The hell with this. I'm off, Frankie.

Emma

I see you run past the health centre and jump the low wall into the Den. I don't shout but, on impulse, I follow you.

Jenny

I see you walking along the floor of the Den. No Joanne. Brilliant.

Joanne

I see you from the ridge on the other side of the Den as I'm turning off for my house. I'm sure that's Jennifer Sim on the path above you. From this angle, it looks like she's standing on your head. Like you're acrobats trying some dangerous act for the first time, out of sight of the public.

That end of the Den narrows and thickens seductively. The foliage is dense. The smell is damp and musty. It's the way to Jenny's house.

Further in there is an old fly-blown iron bridge, where Emma and I used to hold hands and spit into the water.

Emma

I see you sitting in the playpark. It's not as good as the one on the boulevard but it's much quieter so I understand why you're there. I spot Jenny Sim watching you. Back and forward you swing, showing off how high you can get.

Showing off for her.

Joanne

Desperately trying to fly and getting nowhere. I'll miss you though.

Emma

I'm going home. I've got to get out of this damned town. You never forget your first love but it doesn't make them any less of a dick.

Jenny

I should just go down there. It's only a few short steps. Say 'fuck it' and go down and sit on your knee and kiss you. But I'm too scared.

Yesterfield 2023

'Hey, pal!' A teenage girl is watching him. 'You not a bit old to be sitting on swings?'

She has thick black eyeliner and baggy black jeans covered in straps and buckles. She looks a bit like the punk rockers of old. Yet it's still a small town, after all, so she's wearing trainers because there's nowhere to buy proper chunky boots.

'I was waiting for someone.' The man flicks his cigarette expertly into the bushes. 'But I don't think she's coming.'

The girl looks disinterestedly at her watch.

'When were you meant to meet her?'

The man puts his feet on the ground and stops the swing. Motionless, he is still vaguely handsome but his hair is thinning and his features lined and rather pasty.

'1981.'

The girl isn't listening. She has spotted a long-haired boy at the other end of the esplanade and runs towards him, waving.

Her strappy black trousers flap like the wings of a gull and she screeches a welcome in much the same fashion.

'Kids,' the man says without a trace of emotion.

And then, she's there. She wears a long suede coat and matching gloves. Her leather boots look both foreign and expensive.

'Hey, stranger.' She sits down next to him. 'Never thought I'd hear from you again.'

'Didn't expect you to answer my email.' A big, stupid grin splits his face. She remembers it well. He glances sideways at her.

'You look good.' It's true, though he's astonished to see her hair is pure white.

'I know.'

'Been following you on Facebook. You've done well.' He looks around. 'Why did you pick here of all places?'

The petrels scream in indignation, hovering over the car park where Vissocchi's used to stand.

'Only bit I still recognise. I hear the Den's a housing estate now.' She shrugs. 'What would you like to do?'

The sea crashes on the rocks. He takes a deep breath and bites his lip. Pats his knees nervously. It reminds her of a lost child and what he says next only reinforces that.

'I suppose starting again is out of the question?' he jokes.

She laughs, despite herself. They are not the same people and no longer know each other, if they ever did. Have no idea what real triumphs or damage the years have visited, so the question is bold and quaint and careless and silly. All the things she liked about him and all the things she didn't.

'Fuck it.' She gets up and he makes to rise too, unsure of how to act. With a shake of the head, she straddles him and kisses him on the lips.

'Holy shit.' He looks shocked and delighted.

She is shocked and delighted too—not just by his reaction but her own daring. For a long time she has felt like a shadow of her former self and senses he is the same. The sun breaks briefly through the clouds and the light is bright and unforgiving, illuminating every line. Yet, they last met when they were both young and, in some small way, it's how they'll always see each other. Knowing this, Yesterfield transforms into a place of possibilities rather than a prison. Age becomes experience. Life is an adventure. The past moves closer and the future recedes.

It's never too late to keep an unfulfilled promise, she thinks.

'A stroll down memory lane is a lot more exciting when you and I are the only familiar landmarks.' She struggles up and pats his cheek. 'Fancy a walk?'

'Christ, you make me feel like a teenager again,' he laughs. 'Are we going to hold hands?'

'I'll consider it.' She pulls him to his feet and winks. 'Wouldn't want to rush things, though, would we?'

HAPPY ENDINGS

charmaine clancy

Maya

I came for the sex tips. I remind myself that, as the fourth person stands to detail my lack of physical attraction.

'Maya's story shows potential, but I just didn't *feel* it. There's no spark, no *passion*. There's more steam in my bifocals on a warm day than in her romance scene.'

My forced grin wobbles. *Look grateful*. I nod. As if Agatha, in her eighties, sporting red lipstick smeared into surrounding cracks, was bestowing a great gift upon me.

Agatha peers over those bifocals, right at me. 'It was sad. I don't think the female protagonist even orgasmed in that sex scene. Have you ever orgasmed, Maya?'

Oh. My. God.

So, seated amongst almost sixty other writers at the annual Romance Writing Retreat, in Mount Tamborine's Lovewood Lodges,

I ponder my utter lack of charisma and sexual appeal for the third time in my life. I hoped the retreat would live up to this year's theme 'Happy Endings' because the beginning was torture.

Why are we opening with critiques anyway? Last year we kicked off with morning-champagne and macarons. Not that I want a reminder of last year.

Blake stands up next.

No, no, no. I sink lower into my chair and stare at my hands.

'Harsh, Agatha. No doubt, the sex was god damn awful, but I think Maya is hiding a wild side that I would like to see.'

A woman near him cackles.

I should write horror instead.

I mean, I've had sex. And I love romance. Even if it slightly terrifies me. I used to believe it was a type of magic.

As a kid, I searched for four-leaf clovers, made wishes into dandelion breaths and, when I was eight, I was convinced catching the bouquet at Aunty Jean's wedding meant Bradly Jones would propose to me at school the following Monday. He did not. Instead, when I raised the idea of marriage, he said, *Eww, you want me to have sex with you?*

That was the first time I thought I wasn't pretty enough for love. It wasn't the last.

I still love romance stories and find myself hoping and ready in real life for a stranger to spill coffee on me, reach for the same book in a quaint little store, or say —

'Is this seat taken?'

Cormac

It's my own fault for arriving late. The conference is a lot more crowded than it deserves to be with a theme name like 'Happy Endings'.

Figured I could sneak in, capture photographic evidence of my relaxation and recovery, then duck out to touch base with Jackson and see where we're at with the open cases. But now, as I stand by the only empty seat, instead of answering, the woman beside it forms a small 'oh' with her lips. A deep flush of pink overtakes her dimpled cheeks. She dips her face, hiding beneath the mop of deep red curls.

She does not object. I sit.

From the far side of the room, a guy outlines all the reasons a woman can lack sexuality. Weird. Maybe the clients are filing under the grounds of non-compatibility?

He becomes graphically specific.

I lean into my neighbour. 'Ouch. Whoever he's talking about should've lodged a non-disclosure agreement for their physical intimacy.'

The flush spreads right down her neck now. *Oh. I'm an idiot.*

I stand. 'Have to say, I've come across plenty of precedents that suggest the client who complains about poor sex in the union is the one who is deficient in skill.' I sit.

Her hands cover her face and she opens two fingers to peek out. 'What ... what are you doing?'

I nod towards the nob who just finished insulting the plaintiff. He's still standing, mouth as open as those clowns at carnivals waiting to have ping pong balls popped inside. 'Lazy lawyers make personal attacks. Any judge would be furious with his approach.'

57

Her hands drop and her brows push together. 'Huh? What lawyers?'

Why did my office think this would be relaxing for me? These people are more frustrating than the pile of files crowding my in-tray. *Inhale, exhale. Slow it all down.* 'All of you. This is a divorce lawyers' retreat.'

'No. This is a romance writers' retreat.'

Wait, what? I turn in my seat. Everyone is either on a laptop or writing in open notebook. But I saw the sign out front. It sinks in. 'Happy Endings?'

'Yes, that's the theme this year.' She beams and I'm mesmerised by cute little dimples in her freckled cheeks. 'Every romance needs a happy ending.'

What are the odds?

'Okay, if this is romance, then I'm definitely in the wrong place. Feel like an atheist in church.'

'You don't believe in happily-ever-after?'

I shrug. 'I work on the other endings.'

'Horror?'

'Divorce proceedings.'

She smiles and shakes her head, those red curls each choose their own direction to travel. 'Okay, but I'm sure you've been in love.'

'My heart is heavily guarded by terms and conditions.' I rise and smack a palm against my chest in pledge.

On my way out, I lean down to the big doofus who criticised my neighbour's sex scene.

'By the way, she's got plenty of sexuality, maybe you weren't pressing the right buttons.' I give him a short pat on the back, look up to see Miss Dimples smirking and give her a wink.

Maya

Her palm pressed firmly against his broad chest. Locking eyes with his deep blues, she moved her palm down, over his ribs, down, over his abs, down ... daring him to stop her. He didn't.

Brilliant. Well, no, but an improvement on my first draft. Inspiration enthused me. Ally Casswell's workshop on the stages of touching opened my eyes to possibilities. It didn't hurt that I'd envisioned my male protagonist as one charming, albeit confusing, divorce lawyer with grey-blue eyes.

'Maya?'

'Hmm?' My mind pauses with that imaginary hand wavering just over his ... 'Oh, Blake.'

His tousled hair and designer stubble exude an air of effortless confidence. 'We're done for the day, walk with me to the bar for a predinner drink?'

A flash of memory burns my cheeks. 'I, uh, was, uh ... okay.' The last word comes out somewhere between a croak and a squeak.

He flashes that winning smile that always melts me.

As we stroll from the conference room to the main building, he leans down. 'Maya, that fellow you've brought along has me worried,' He elbows me softly and winks, 'I might have missed my chance.'

I'd wanted his attention for the past three years that I've attended this retreat. He smiles now, as though I'm attractive. My body feels instantly fatter, my face uglier. My every movement is like fumbling to catch a live fish wearing oven mitts.

When I don't respond, he adds, 'Are you two serious?'

'Me? I ... what? Who?'

'The guy who gave me a mouthful for criticising your sex scene.'

'What? Oh, no. No.' He thought that lawyer was *with* me? Cormac. I remember the name scrawled on his name tag. As if he'd be dating someone who looks like I do.

As if Blake would.

'Good. Then I do still stand a chance.' He holds the wide glass door open for me.

'Blake, Blake!' Olivia, the cackler, waves from a barstool. 'I saved you a seat.'

As soon as we approach, her hand reaches out to touch his arm as if it's not the scariest thing to do in the world.

'Okay girls, what'll it be?' Blake beckons the woman behind the bar, run off her feet between the romance writers and lawyers all ordering rounds.

I spot Cormac on the other side of the bar. His back is to me and he appears to be sharing a story with a large group. Probably laughing at the stupid romance writer who sucks at writing romance.

'Ooh, something pink and naughty for me.' Olivia's boobs jiggle in time with her giggles. 'Do you drink alcohol Maya? Get her a juice, Blake.'

'Sorry, what's that?' Blake leans down after I've mumbled.

I clear my throat. 'Double shot of tequila.'

Cormac

This is not relaxing. I've been all over this bloody mountain lodge resort and I can't pick up phone reception anywhere. Not true, actually. I get one bar when I balance between the second and third step to my cabin, but I only get about three seconds into the call, and it cuts out.

All through today's conference, my head swarmed with thoughts of work. The files that need lodging for the Sullivan case, Mrs Van der Meer's bakery — she'll lose if her husband puts an injunction on her bank account — and gaining access to shared funds for Ms Lowe so she can pay her daughter's tuition.

I've had more stress not working than I would any day in the office. Well, okay, not counting last Tuesday, when I collapsed. But taking time off was a poor prescription. The only time I relaxed at all today was in that other group's retreat, when the cute writer, Maya, distracted me. And the fifty or so times she popped into my mind throughout the day.

And there she is.

Across the bar. She just tipped back a shot. And now she's spluttering. How is this so adorable?

'Excuse me.' Before I have time to think this through, I weave through the Happy Endings lawyers and into the Happy Endings writers.

Maya

Agatha has me cornered.

'Dating apps are ruining romance. Back in my day, he'd spot you at a dance, walking down the street, or in the supermarket and his best

61

friend would ask outright if you wanted to go steady with his buddy. Now the only meet-cutes are swiping right.'

I don't ask how she knows which way to swipe. Agatha is the oldest regular attendee at these retreats but she's also the most published.

I crane my neck to locate Blake. *Oh.* Olivia is cosying up to him in a corner.

'So, have you written any hot romances featuring a divorce lawyer?' It's Cormac.

'Oh, honey, the minute I put a lawyer in my stories they have less spark than a soggy firecracker.' Agatha's quip gets a laugh from Cormac, and I wish, just wish, I had the ability to speak so freely. She never gets embarrassed.

Cormac turns to me. I'm not sure if it was the shots I'd already had or that I wanted to appear brave in front of Agatha, but I'm oddly comfortable speaking up. 'You don't want to appear in my manuscripts, I suck. My characters lack chemistry, probably because I flunked science in high school.'

He smirks.

'Besides,' I continue, 'how would you even have a meet-cute? Not very romantic if your character is in the midst of a divorce.'

'True. I can't help with a meet-cute, only a leave-ugly.'

Agatha leant in and whispered, 'I think you've finally found your spark.' And she sailed off, leaving us alone. Alone in a crowded bar.

Cormac

Agatha's departure leaves us in a bubble of sorts, shielded from the noise and chatter around us. A strange sense of ease settles over me, one that I can't attribute solely to the alcohol.

'Leave-ugly, huh?' She raises an eyebrow, a playful sparkle in her eyes.

I shrug. 'Hey, a divorce lawyer's gotta have some tricks up their sleeve, right?'

There's a lull and I do that thing my mother keeps telling me to stop, I say exactly what's on my mind. 'You're the most fun I've had in a long time.'

Maya's cheeks flush, and she looks away. 'Thanks. You seem to be the only one here who doesn't see me as a walking disaster.'

I shake my head, a smirk tugging at the corner of my mouth. 'Walking disaster? I've seen far worse.'

Her eyes narrow. 'Well, I appreciate the vote of confidence, Mr Prenup Protector.'

I chuckle. 'Genuinely, you are the only person here who has been able to distract me from the fact I cannot get Wi-Fi or reception anywhere on this mountain.'

'Huh, I get reception in my room.'

'Are you trying to lure me?'

Her giggle tickles me.

I thumb in the direction of the corner. 'I saw the doofus with the big mouth ogling you earlier, he keeps looking over. What's that about?'

She shakes her head. 'Just one of my many romantic mistakes.'

I raise a brow, 'Okay, many.'

She slaps my chest. 'No, not like that! I mean I get my hopes up and then ruin it with my ...' she waves to her whole self.

'Your what?'

'My, I don't know, *me-ness*.'

The barmaid comes around and I order a beer, when I raise an eye to Maya, she says 'same', so I make it a jug.

I turn back to Maya.

'Are you crazy? You are fun! Fun and funny, and smart.' *And pretty*, but I don't say that, because this amazing girl is showing me friendship and I don't want to make it weird. 'Maybe you're aiming at the wrong doofuses?'

The dimples make a reappearance. 'Thanks for the advice, but you don't even believe in romance.'

'True love is a myth and romance novels are just fairy tales for grown-ups. But we can put it to the test if you like.'

Maya

My eyes widen and my cheeks burn but I remind myself Cormac is not suggesting anything dirty. He said it himself, fun, funny, smart. *Not hot or sexy.* He doesn't see me that way. Because even when I try to be, I'm not.

Still, this is easy, spending time with Cormac. I'd being lying if I didn't admit he is outrageously sexy with that hair, those eyes and that oh-so-firm chest. I bet he's never eaten a whole tub of Neapolitan ice-cream for breakfast.

'What are you suggesting? You want me to make doofus—I mean, Blake, his name is Blake—fall in love with me?'

He rubs his chin and looks over at Blake. Blake is staring back at us.

'No. Just show me one couple who can convince me there is even the potential for true, eternal love and you win.'

'Hmm, what do I win?'

'You won't, true love is a hoax, but prove me wrong, and I'll write you a sonnet and read it in front of everyone at your retreat.'

Okay, I like that idea. 'Wait, how do I know that's even a challenge for you? Maybe you pen sonnets in your spare time.'

'Fair question, but firstly, I have no spare time, and secondly, here's a sample of my poetry prowess, Roses are red, violets are blue, I'm a divorce lawyer ... so this poem's not for you.'

He throws his hands up in the air to emphasise the tragedy of his attempt.

I can't hold in my giggles. 'And if I lose?'

'We swap rooms. I get your good, good phone reception.'

Cormac

She starts with Agatha. Shy Maya bursts out of her shell and almost drags the old woman back over.

'Really, you two, you can't have run out of things to talk about already.'

When Maya quizzes Agatha about her past romances, Agatha happily discloses lurid details of liaisons and grand gestures. Maya pushes about which of the many, many men Agatha named was her 'true love.'

'True love? Ha! Never found it, and I was married seven times.'

Maya questions whether there is someone new on the horizon.

'Sweetie, the only spice I get a whiff of these days is Old Spice.'

Next, I'm led over to meet a woman who apparently bases all her romance novels on her husband. It bursts Maya's bubble to learn she is getting a divorce. I ask if she had a prenup and discretely pass my business card before we head back to the bar.

That Blake guy sidles up next to her and leans down to talk close to her face. She orders us a couple of cocktails the same pink shade as her cheeks.

'Hey, how about we ask your doofus friend?' I nod to Blake who is now back working the blonde sitting next to him.

'No! I mean, we aren't close … I … uh …' One minute near him and she is all awkward and shy again. I decide I dislike this guy. A lot.

'Okay, Maya, spill, who is this dude to you?'

She hesitates and I can see her mind going to an uncomfortable memory. 'We … crossed paths last year.'

I arch an eyebrow. 'Crossed paths? Care to elaborate?'

Maya clears her throat, avoiding my gaze. 'Let's just say it was an interesting encounter and one I'd rather forget.'

'You've piqued my curiosity.'

'Not something I care to relive or share.'

My blood pounds in my temples. I know what my doctor would say. But if this guy … I barely get out through gritted teeth. 'Did he … *hurt* you?'

'I don't know, kind of?' Then her eyes grow wide. 'Oh, no, not like that! Look, I'll tell you, just please don't laugh.' She glances about. 'It started last year, no, I guess it started with Steve about eight years ago. Or Bradly in grade three.'

One of the women from the divorce lawyers' retreat staggers toward us carrying five Coronas. Maya shuts down and looks to her feet.

'Coooormac! You mush join us, we are shela- shela-brahing. Here.' She shoves a bottle at me and it splashes over my shirt. 'You too.' She pops one on the table next to Maya. Then she staggers off again.

Maya

I start with my botched proposal in grade four, and when Cormac doesn't make fun of me, I move on to Steve, the boyfriend I'd lived with at Uni. The one who told me he loved me but couldn't keep pretending to be attracted to me. The one who suggested I lose weight and cover my freckles. And because once I start, I can't stop, I tell him about last year's encounter with Blake. 'I thought he was flirting with me, but I'd been too shy all these years. So, in a late-night moment, I figured, why not?'

'Because I respect you, I won't list the reasons.'

I grin at that, Cormac puts me at ease, even when I'm sharing my worst mistakes. 'Anyhow, I rocked up at his room around midnight, and knocked on his door. When he didn't answer, I dragged a bin to his bedroom window and climbed up to wake him. He was awake. He just wasn't alone. When I tried to retreat, I fell off the bin and both he and Lisa ... Lisa Lee, you may have heard of her? She writes all those outback romances?'

He shrugs and shakes his head.

'Oh wow, her face is everywhere. Like literally in every book shop. Well, they came out in time to see me limp away.'

'Ouch.'

'Yep. Now Blake knows I had a huge crush.'

'Presumptuous of him, maybe you were there for Lisa, I mean, her face is everywhere.'

It's so easy to laugh with Cormac.

'Maya.' Blake's smooth voice right behind me makes me jump. 'Woah, it's okay.' He steps up against me and places his hands on my hips. A lump grows in my throat. I don't know whether to talk to him over my shoulder or turn and face him. But he's touching me and if I turn around, we'll be right up against each other and ... and ...

Instead, I slide out of his grip, take a step forward and then turn.

'Hi, Blake Reed, romance author.' He shoves out a hand at Cormac.

Cormac creases his brow, looks to me, and then to Blake, but does not offer his hand. 'Yeah, Cormac Duffy, court document author.'

Blake nods, as if this makes perfect sense. He steps to my side and puts an arm around my shoulders. I shrink.

Cormac's brows fuse. He excuses himself and wanders back over to the lawyers' side of the room.

Cormac

It's what she wants. She'd said that. She has a crush on that man. No point in me hanging around.

Besides, if I wanted to spend an evening chatting to entertaining women, they outnumber men about three to one over at the lawyers' conference. But. They're not Maya.

Had. She said she'd *had* a huge crush on Blake. Not has, had. I rush back.

She is standing alone.

I pause, not daring to get too close.

She smiles. 'You came back.'

I shrug, 'I really want that room.'

She laughs and it's magnificent. Then she takes my hand. 'Come on then, I'll let you share my good, good, phone reception.'

But I don't end up making any calls ...

Maya

The morning sun stings my eyelids. I rouse and wonder at the weight across me. Cormac's arm.

We had laughed and talked and laughed. He'd asked permission before reaching out for me and I had given it. I'd forgotten about Blake, about Bradley Jones, even Steve. What I *do* remember is Cormac's opinion of romance.

He'd been honest. The passion and flesh of last night changes nothing. He specialises in break-ups, not love. He doesn't even believe in it.

Maybe I don't either.

Slipping from his big spoon, I silently slip on jeans and a Happy Endings shirt. Soft rumbling snores come from his side of the bed. I pack my bag and take his room key from the pocket of his pants. Before I exit the front door, I leave a note by the microwave.

You win. The room is yours.

Cormac

She's gone.

You win. There is no victory for me. Just a suitcase of my belongings delivered by the concierge.

I pick up my phone. Two bars. Just past eight-thirty. Jackson will be in the office, I could check in. Instead, I open the notes app and type up a different kind of prenup. It is poorly drafted. Actually, it's woeful, but it's the best I have.

The conference is in full swing by the time I arrive.

She's there. Not *just* there, Maya is standing up in front of her entire Happy Endings retreat and she's reading her work to them. *Wow.* I love seeing her like this.

I slip into the back and listen. I don't know much about romance novels, but this is impressive writing. I'm not the only one who thinks so. The group explodes with applause.

Agatha stands and mocks fanning herself. 'With a flush like this, I could win a round of poker. Maya that was brave and beautiful. Well done.'

Maya's gorgeous blush is back and she turns to her seat.

Her eyes catch me.

Agatha turns to the audience. 'Is there anyone else who would like to read their work?'

I step forward.

Maya

He's here? And not just here, he's stepping up to speak.

He clears his throat. Is he sweating?

'Um, this is titled *I Lost a Bet.*'

He scrolls through his phone, finds what he's looking for and reads.

'*Love is but a fairy tale for grown-ups,*
An untruth, whispered by fools in 'I do.'
I believed this, when I drafted prenups.'

He looks up at me and shrugs.

'I am not a romance writer, that's you.
I often crafted terms, cold and precise,
I could not think I'd feel a love that's true,
But in your eyes, my cynic heart did splice.
This divorce lawyer's sonnet is for you.

You could hate me, but I would hate me more,
if I should be the cause that we must part,
Only one asset's loss could make me poor,
You have it now, completely, it's my heart.
Your claim, true love exists, was right you see,
Here stands the proof, spoiler alert, it's me.'

There are a few awkward claps. His face turns beetroot.

I don't remember standing but find myself weaving between tables to get to him.

'Um, fair, it is bloody awful. Maya, I know you're searching for a knight in shining armour, but …'

I reach up and clutch his shirt in my fists. 'Who needs a knight in shining armour, I'd rather my lawyer in a shiny suit.' I pull him down to my lips.

Now they really applaud.

BREWING LOVE

chris radge

Day two at the Pet Café and the sensory overload threatened to splinter Olivia's mind. She could handle the aroma of the spicy local coffee that sat on the back of her tongue and the usual chatter over a coffee. But the barrage of barking dogs with their doggy breaths, meowing cats, and never-ending condolences was the catalyst that would do her head in.

One saving grace was heading home next door, to the quaint rural-style cottage with its pristine white siding and inviting front verandah. She imagined Grams sitting on one of the twin rocking chairs only a week ago, decompressing the long day.

Olivia had inherited the pet café, PetSteP, and moved into the adjoining residence yesterday. Her meagre possessions lined up hard up against the wall of the spotless lounge room. She didn't own many tangible belongings. He'd seen to that. She shook her head, trying to shake *him* from her mind.

Breathing deep she centred herself.

I can do this.

The pet café was her sanctuary now. She had to sate the needs of these country folk, and for the memory of her Grams.

She glanced at the mounting coffee orders and served up another plate of specialised dog biscuits for the furries, and warm scones and jam for their best friends. She knew the hustle and bustle of this fast paced café would take her mind off everything. Here is where she needed to be.

'Liv, we're down to a dozen of Grams' prized Pumpkin Pet biscuits, and only six of the Umami ones,' said Zoey, her barista and best friend from high school. 'We need to find those recipes, and fast.'

'Is there an actual recipe book?'

'Not that I've noticed. Grams always had a batch of biscuits cooling in the kitchen when I arrived in the morning.' She smiled sliding a coffee to a waiting customer. 'There is a scone recipe taped to the shelf in the kitchen. It was my first job in the morning while Grams did paperwork.'

Olivia nodded as she fumbled with the coffee machine that looked more like a stainless-steel church organ pumping out dreams and ideas, promising an awakening for those who drank from it.

One thing at a time, Olivia thought.

'Damn it,' she whispered through clenched teeth, and ran cold water over her second steam burn that morning. The blistering pain was nothing compared to the heartache of coming home and knowing she would never see Grams again. And just for a moment she wished she was back in the big smoke running numbers, secure in her corporate accounting job. But she had to leave that world. Needed to get out of that toxic relationship and put him, Daniel, behind her.

Olivia realised now, she'd been nothing but arm candy, a way to the top for Daniel. But to find *him*, and her boss in *their bed*, had tipped her over the edge, mangled her mind.

She could have dealt with that. Could have shut him out of her life, but her Grams' death that same day, had shattered her into a jigsaw of emotions, ripping a bottomless hole in her heart.

She no longer gave a horseshit about Daniel, her now ex-fiancé, but the damage he'd inflicted was too great. She recognised his controlling ways now. Knew what would be coming next. The dozens of delivered flowers, the expensive gifts he had paid for with her credit card. He'd say the words her heart wanted to hear, and she would have inevitably fallen back into his arms. Not this time. Not a chance. But it didn't stop her keeping one wary eye on the front door.

She swiped at the *poor me* tears with the back of her hand and remembered the satisfaction of cancelling the credit card with its unanswered charges.

'You okay?' said Zoey, worry creasing her brows.

'Yep.' She was good at pushing things aside, an expert in fact. 'That espresso steam blaster is crazy-hot.'

'Took me months to figure it out.' Zoey glanced at her new boss.

Zoey had been the girl Olivia had shared her deepest secrets with once, her confidant, her sounding board. It was nice to have a best friend back in her life.

'Olivia!' Zoey nudged her from the spiralling memories. She looked up to see the local priest next in line, behind him the customers gathered around a commotion at the café entrance.

'I'm sorry Father, I need to make sure nobody is hurt.'

'It's all right child.' He adjusted his clerical collar. 'I can wait for this morning's cup of enlightenment. Your blend is a religious experience I look forward to every day.'

Warmth caressed the gleam in her eyes. She left the half-made coffee and went to investigate as the clergyman followed.

She stood on tippy toes trying to see better from the edge of the crowd. There, in the middle of the gathering, knelt a tall dark-haired man with his back to her. A miniature Pomeranian fluff ball lay prone in front of him, fitting uncontrollably in the reflective colours from the stained-glass window, its long pink tongue lolling from the side of its mouth.

'Excuse me ladies, gents.' The stranger's deep velvety voice rolled over her like a wave, leaving Olivia with a strange fluttering in her chest. 'Let's give little Flossy some room.'

Olivia nudged her way through the milling crowd. She wasn't exactly sure what she'd find when she got there. She knew CPR, but that wouldn't help. She stood helpless and watched as Zoey knelt next to him, their backs to her. Olivia's eyes widened at the sight of the dark hair at the nape of the stranger's neck. Curls that had once made her teenage heart leap when she'd sat behind them in class. Curls she'd wanted to wrap around her finger.

Curls she wanted to mess up and run her fingers through, grab and tug as she kissed those perfect lips.

'Settle Gretel,' she mumbled to herself. *It can't be him. He left right after graduation without so as much as a goodbye.*

The stranger's toned muscles rippled beneath his well fitted shirt. His sleeves evenly rolled up showing off tanned forearms. Her eyes travelled down the length of his body. Desire burnt her empty heart and in places she thought would be dead forever. The rhythm and movement promising things, thoughts she shouldn't be having while this stranger was saving a furry customer's life.

Zoey squeezed the man's shoulder in a familiar gesture exchanging glances, and leant in close whispering something, smiling, like they'd done this before.

He's Zoey's boyfriend? Olivia snapped back to reality.

'Flossy will be fine now Mrs Hendy,' the stranger said, 'We will do some follow-up tests when you come in for her appointment this afternoon.' He handed the pooch to the worried owner. 'Thanks for the assist, Z.' He pecked her on the cheek.

Olivia's pulse flip-flopped, as her mind raced with a mix of emotions. How did this man know Zoey's nickname? Only one other person called her Z and—

He turned to face Olivia.

'You.' She wanted to hide in a corner and disappear, remembering the feelings from moments before, but her legs refused to move. Ethan, with the perfect combination of athleticism and intelligence, had always fascinated her. But he never seemed to notice her that way at school, and besides, he and Zoey were together now, any fool could see that. The touches, the kiss on the cheek. And to top it off, they had made a best friends pact when they were ten. The untouchable friends zone. It had seared her budding teenage heart then, and stabbed at it now.

'Olivia?' Ethan's recognition carried a mix of surprise and delight.

She nodded, her words caught in her throat as she smoothed out her coffee-stained apron, willing her brain to work, her mouth to speak.

Here, standing smack bang in front of her, was her high-school crush, and the third part of their best friend pack. All cohesive thought was lost, gone, and this career-driven woman had been reduced to a teenager in a matter of moments.

'It's been a while.' He reached out and placed a comforting hand on her shoulder.

She squirmed under his touch and blurted, 'You. Here?'

'I'm the Vet next door.' A warm smile tugged at Ethan's lips.

'Didn't you, um leave?'

'I did,' he said gently. 'University.'

She just nodded.

'I didn't expect to find you here running the pet café.' He moved a little closer. 'Weren't you headed for the big smoke?'

'I was. I did. Stuff happened.' She shrugged wishing she'd taken more care in the mirror that morning.

'I'm sorry about Grams.' He blinked away the glassiness in his eyes, his thumb lightly brushed across her flesh in a caring gesture.

Tentacles of teenage desire shot down her spine, reigniting fifteen-year-old Olivia's crush. But this was wrong, he was someone else's now. She had to change the subject. Had to stop the memories. Her moment, though long ago, had been missed. Those times when a look wasn't enough.

She shrugged off his hand and stepped away yabbering to herself in a quiet voice.

'Of course, he would visit Grams. They were practically neighbours, and everybody needs coffee.'

'You know I can hear you,' he said in a gentle voice.

'What. You can?' Her school yard insecurities crept back.

He nodded trying not to grin. Almost every head in the café turned their way. He put an arm around Olivia and guided her towards Grams' tiny office.

'Let's go in here.' Ethan suggested. 'This town can be such a busy-body crowd sometimes.'

'What about the coffees? The biscuits? The Priest's order?'

'I'm sure Z has everything under control. She'll be fine. Besides we will be right here if it gets too crazy.' He closed the door to the bright office, only meant for one.

Sinking into the plush office chair, Olivia took a deep calming breath, feeling a mix of frustration, exhaustion, and the weight of her Grams' legacy pressing down on her shoulders and these renewed feelings she was struggling to push aside.

'My life is such a mess,' Olivia mumbled, her voice tinged with desperation and self-doubt. 'How is a corporate accountant supposed to run a café for humans and their besties?' She looked around the tiny office for answers that just weren't there.

'I know we haven't seen each other for years, but I still believe you're the same go-getter girl I knew growing up.' He leant against the office door.

'I'm more used to sitting in front of a desk.' She swivelled around in the office chair, arms wide. 'Like this one.'

'You'll be fine.'

'How do you even know that?' she spat out in a crazed questioning voice.

'I know because you've, we've done it before.'

'You know, when we were ten and had that dog biscuit stall out the front of your Grams' place trying to raise money for our school excursion.'

The memory crashed into her, winding her response.

It was the moment she realised she'd liked Ethan, but he'd been an oblivious boy. The memories of getting in trouble constantly for daydreaming about him in class, not doing her chores, not being able to sleep. Most of all, the many hours the three best friends worked on perfecting the recipes.

'The recipes!' She jumped from her chair slamming into Ethan's rock-hard chest. Embarrassment and tingles shot down her spine as their eyes met.

'Steady on Liv.' A smile played at his lips as he steadied her taking care not to grab the earlier steam burn.

'Um, sorry.' Her old insecurities seeped back. 'Do you remember any of those recipes?' She mentally crossed everything.

'Possibly. What do you reckon we brain storm this after work?'

'Perfect, let's say six in the café kitchen.'

She took one last look around the well-organised office, the walls neatly covered in photos and nostalgia, except for one on her desk. An old photograph of Grams, Zoey, Ethan and her, arms linked, with flour-dusted aprons. The memories of baking together, her Grams' warm embrace, and the love they shared. She plucked the photo from the desk, and hugged it. Embarrassment licked at her conscious, wondering if he thought she was hugging him, and shoved it into her apron.

'Do you want to pick up some pizza on the way?'

'One thing I'm good at doing, and that's ordering take out.'

Dinner with Ethan. Olivia's heart betrayed her again.

'I'll swing round and pick up Z, three memories are better than two.'

And that same heart flopped into her steel toed, non-slip boots.

'Olivia,' Zoey called out.

'Gotta go.' She tried to push past him but could see it was near impossible in the small office. They'd have to do a tricky tango step, bodies plastered together, faces inches away. Hyperaware of her predicament, she mumbled, 'I need to get past you.'

'I've got patients to see myself.' He grinned grabbing for the door handle. 'See you tonight?'

'Hmm.'

He left the office with the intoxicating scent of warm male spice lingering in the small space clouding her thoughts. She breathed deep, head giddy. No. She had to stop. This was not a man she could have feelings for. He was taken, spoken for, out of reach.

Red wine and pizza sauce marred the butcher paper scribblings.

'I think we've nailed it,' Ethan said chomping on his cheesy crust. 'The only way we can really know, is to make these peanut-butter doggy biscuits.'

'Not tonight, I'm spent,' said Zoey, 'A girl needs her beauty rest.'

Olivia watched Ethan rest a comforting hand on Zoey's shoulder. Jealousy niggled at her, but these were her best friends. She should be happy for them, right?

'I'll zip you home,' Ethan said, 'but first ...' He reached for a tea-towel. '... we need to clean up.'

'Just leave it. I'll clean it up in the morn—.' Olivia reached for the same tea-towel. Their fingers brushing. Neither moved or said a word.

'Come on you two.'

Zoey's laugh broke Olivia from her spiralling feelings, pulling her hand away like it'd been stung.

'I'll help tomorrow.' Zoey yawned.

Olivia looked up to see Ethan studying her. His smouldering dark eyes surrendering a love she was not sure was there, and looked away.

Was this thing real between Zoey and Ethan?

Olivia considered had asking Zoey about her relationship with Ethan. That's what best friends did, right? But the heady red wine had flowed freely, and she'd missed her chance.

'See you in the morning.' She watched her two best friends walk through the front door, doorbell jangling, and locked it behind them.

Olivia's heart on hold again.

It was Saturday, day three, and the morning coffee rush had thinned out.

'Zoey, I forgot to show you this last night.' Olivia pulled out the photo she'd transferred from yesterday's coffee-stained apron already in the washing machine. 'I found a photo of Grams and us three baking. We were ten'.

'That ...' Zoey indicated the photo with the tip of her broom. '... used to be stuck on the cake fridge. Look, the Blu Tack is still there.'

'I think it should go back there.' Olivia felt her Grams' love pulse through her and pushed the photo onto the cold display fridge. But it fluttered to the floor landing face down. She swooped it up quickly not wanting it to get damaged and noticed her Grams' tiny handwriting on the back. 'Zoey.' She waved the photo like a flag. 'Look, on the back. I've found the pumpkin biscuit recipe.'

'Perfect, we only have one of those left.'

'Do you know where Grams kept the ingredients?'

'There's pumpkin puree in the freezer. The rest would be in the kitchen, top shelf.' She motioned still holding the broom. 'Biscuit cutters are in the second draw on the right.'

Olivia pushed the swinging door to the kitchen. 'Might also make a batch of those peanut butter ones we brainstormed last night.'

'I've got you covered.' Zoey grinned indicating towards the almost empty shop. 'But we might need a double batch of both.'

'On it.' Her grin got even wider until the bell above the door rang. She saw Ethan on the other side. Olivia couldn't bear to watch the two love birds and made a B-line for the kitchen.

Olivia pulled the double batch of pumpkin biscuits from the oven and measured the ingredients for the peanut-butter biscuits. The comforting, sweet smell of pumpkin boosted her mood. I *really can do this!* She mentally patted herself on the back until a voice boomed in the stainless-steel kitchen. 'You know, I worked in a bakery when I was putting myself through university.'

'Wha—' The shock sent the bowl of precisely weighed flour she was holding, into a cloud of white rain, leaving the kitchen bench like a dusted-down crime scene.

She cowered against the workbench, waiting for the berating she knew was coming. Daniel, her ex, was always quick to criticise any of her slip ups. She felt a hand on her shoulder, and recoiled.

'It's all right Liv. It's me. Ethan.' His breath permeated the air around them.

'Ethan?' She turned and looked up, her eyes clearing in recognition.

'It's okay, I've got you.' His hand cupped her cheek as he leant in to wipe away the flour dust with his thumb. His touch shuddered her hammering heart.

And in that moment, all memories of her ex-Daniel were pushed aside and the world around her disappeared. A light shiver ran like a wave down her body, her heart was falling. Her lips parted with unspoken words.

'Liv.' Ethan froze for only a moment. Vulnerability cracked his voice. Closing his mouth over hers he gently kissed her.

'Ethan.' She breathed. Her soft tender lips tingled wanting more. More than she dared to believe she had a right to. There's something about a long awaited first kiss that freezes time, sucks the ambient noise into silence.

'Excuse me.' Zoey stood at the kitchen door, hands on hips.

Olivia pushed Ethan from her.

'Z. Oh my god. Sorry.' She fumbled an apology. 'You have every right to—'

'Stop. Ethan out.' She pointed to the door.

He raised his palms in defeat stepping backwards towards the door.

'Z, I didn't mean … It just …' Olivia stammered.

'Liv, it's okay.'

'What.' She looked up dumbfounded. 'But he's your boyfriend.'

Zoey chuckled. 'We're just best friends. The three of us are. We rekindled that when he got back from university. Ethan has been trying to help me. I want to be a vet nurse.'

'The dog, the kiss, the whispering.'

'Ewe, are you crazy. He's always been mad about you. You're all he talks about, has ever talked about.'

Olivia's self-doubt melted away.

The scent of freshly baked dog biscuits wafted through the air, mingling with the aroma of rich coffee and Ethan's musky aftershave. She'd managed to find Grams' Umami recipe, laminated and taped securely to the bottom of a large biscuit bottle sitting on the front counter. But their combined skill in baking, hers in accounting, and Ethan's veterinary knowledge offered the possibility of a new business venture together.

'Liv, I've been thinking about us, about high school. I didn't really understand what love was then. I wish I'd stopped and listened to my own heart.'

Olivia's breath caught in her throat as Ethan cupped her face.

His kiss was feather light. But she wanted more, needed more. His gaze held an intensity she couldn't ignore, filled with the same longing she felt deep within her soul, easing any doubt or hesitations she had.

'Ethan, I feel the same way. The feelings I once felt for you are still very much alive. Ethan, I—'

Just as Olivia was beginning to open her heart to the possibility of being with Ethan forever, her past stormed through the front door of the café. Her ex-fiancé stood before her, arms laden with two dozen long-stem red roses, and a rather large Louis Vuitton bag swinging from his fingertips.

She felt Ethan stiffen beside her.

'Daniel?' she stammered, her brain numb with shock. Panic clawed at her as she pushed away from the table splashing the freshly made coffees trying to get as far away from him as possible.

Almost instantly her mind was trapped in a familiar narcissistic cage, disintegrating her mind, regressing to a time when Daniel's passionate kisses had made sense and ruled her every move. Their three-year engagement with no wedding date, had left her with nothing but a broken heart. Head bent in submission, she noticed the reflection of the stained glass window on the floor. It was enough to break her from the trance and remind her where she was.

Wipe away those tears sweetheart, her Grams would say, *chin up, shoulders back and get on with it.*

Grams inheritance was a lifeline, a chance for a fresh start. In that moment, she knew that chapter of her life was really over, and she reached for the grounding of Ethan's touch.

'I love you, Olivia.' Daniel's laser-like stare made her squirm in disgust.

'Leave.' Using her best steely stare, she kept her responses brief to the gaslighting narcissist.

'You won't be able to make it without me.' He smirked back at her.

'I already have.' She saw the first crack in his armour appear as the Vuitton bag stopped swinging.

'You know I don't love her, never loved her.' He spread his arms wide like he was addressing a crowd.

'I'm not willing to talk about this. Now, leave.' A tremor in her hand threatened her resolve as she stabbed a finger towards the door.

'But—'

She moved towards the sanctuary of her Grams' office pulling Ethan with her.

Daniel tried to follow her, roses scattering to the floor, forgotten. He snatched a hand out towards her shoulder.

Ethan stepped between them, as the local police jangled the café's little bell once more.

'She's my fiancée,' said Daniel.

Olivia about faced. 'Not in your wildest dreams. Now leave.'

'You heard the lady,' Ethan said as the local police officer stepped towards Daniel.

'There's a small matter of speeding into town, and an outstanding arrest warrant for aggravated assault,' the officer said slapping cuffs on Daniel's wrists.

Café patrons crowded around her offering their support. She turned her face up to Ethan. 'I feel safe right here,' she said straining on tippy toes to kiss him. 'With you is where I belong.'

A month had passed since Daniel's arrest, and Olivia's life had done a complete three sixty.

Their new dog biscuit business had gone into marketing mode. Stocktaking the pre-packaged dog biscuit, sitting like little parishioners in a church, was mundane but necessary. The café was booming, and their little business had blown up on social media. Tourists came by the droves, bringing their furry best friends for the experience of a menu that sated the hunger of all two- and four-legged friends who ventured in.

But she was distracted.

'You're incorrigible.' She giggled as the love-of-her-life nuzzled at her ear.

'Ethan. People are watching.'

'Let them.'

She turned to face him running her fingers through his curls tugging lightly as she lured his lips to hers.

The blaze of connection that flowed between them gave her the solace and clarity she needed. She was ready to take a chance on a future with Ethan and the path to rediscovering her own strength and voice.

And knew in her soul, they were brewing the perfect love.

MY BIRTHDAY KISS

lizz curry

I paced before the front door, excited with anticipation—not that I would be telling Emily any of this. For weeks, I had insisted that I didn't want her to organise anything for my birthday. I had everything I needed—my cat, my car, my house—what more could one person want?

It had all started when we were out for drinks last Friday. I'd gotten a bit tipsy and accidentally let it slip that I hadn't kissed anyone in the past ten years. Emily had stared at me, horrified.

'Now I know exactly what to get you for your birthday!' she said in triumph.

I'd groaned. Emily had her own unique way of turning everything into a big deal.

'A prostitute!'

'There is no way in hell you are getting me a prostitute.' I hadn't kissed anyone in a decade. Jumping straight into bed with a stranger was another matter entirely.

'Fine.' Emily rolled her eyes at me. 'I guess you just want an old boring cake and card then?'

'And what's wrong with a cake and a card?' I asked. 'And please don't let it be old,' I added cheekily.

'What if I organise a prostitute to just come by and give you a birthday kiss?' When she saw my expression, Emily hastily added, 'And nothing else.'

I remember looking past Emily and noticing that everyone else at the bar were couples, holding hands, whispering sweet nothings, all mocking me with their love. When Emily had a plan, she was like a dog with a bone. And maybe she was right. Maybe I did need a little more excitement in my life. Afterall, the highlight of my week had been finding out that my credit card application had been approved.

And now I was at home on a Monday morning, waiting for a prostitute to come by my house with the special delivery of a birthday kiss. I breathed in deeply, hoping there was a way to calm my fluttering heart and trembling hands. Part of me wanted to call the whole thing off in case I risked a heart attack with all this anxiety, but there was another part of me that couldn't wait for this mystery man to arrive.

When I finally agreed to Emily's plan, I insisted he be roughly my age, and not overwhelmingly handsome. To this, she pulled a face, but I stayed strong. I wanted to feel as if I wasn't kissing someone blessed with rugged good looks, whose only job in life was to please lonely women like me. Emily had laughed, but agreed to my conditions.

92

I reached for my phone to check the time, but it wasn't in my back jeans pocket. In my haste to get ready I'd probably left it on the bed. I wanted to look nice for my kissing prostitute. I got up early to shower and blow-dry my hair. I even put on a bit of makeup and some sweet-scented jasmine perfume. My lips were a pale pink, and my eyelids a subtle shade of gold. I put more effort into my appearance this morning than I had for Friday night drinks with Emily. Looking at my watch, I saw that it was twenty-five past nine. Almost showtime. And then there was a knock at the door.

I immediately stopped pacing and pushed back the waves of hair that had settled on my forehead. Blood rushed to my face, blurring my vision and making me feel lightheaded. I must be blushing. Yet, as I reached for the doorhandle, my hand was steady. This is what I had waited all weekend for. Heck, if I was truly honest with myself, I'd been waiting for this for the better part of a decade.

With my breath caught in my throat, I pulled at the front door and it swung wide open with the help of a salty summer breeze. Standing on my front doorstep was a beautiful man with a rich, dark tan and a crooked smile on his face. Yes, he was my age, but Emily had ignored my request for somebody plain. Now that he was here, I didn't care. He held my birthday card in his hand.

'Tracey?'

His dark brown eyes looked earnestly into mine, and as I returned his stare, my heartrate quickened again. Without knowing what I was doing, I reached for the envelope and tossed it behind my head, into the hallway. I placed my hand on the back of his neck and led his face down to mine. He paused, drawing out the moment it took for our mouths to touch, making me want this with so much more intensity.

And before I knew it, his hand was on the small of my back, gently guiding my body towards his. When his full lips finally met mine, I was in ecstasy. Tiny pinpricks of static energy rippled and ignited upon every touch to my skin. Every subtle action was felt through the light fabric of my top. I became aware of each of his fingertips, affectionately moving and caressing the curves of my body. He was holding me with the tender strength of his arms — warm and comforting and safe.

My hands moved to feel every inch of him that I could reach. His body was toned and muscular, his shoulders broad and strong. My hand moved upwards and I ran my fingers through his thick hair, feeling him become unsteady as I did. And then he held me tighter, and I pushed my body further into his.

Both of his hands gradually made their way up my body, resting on my neck and then delicately cupping each side of my face. His spiced scent mixed with the jasmine on my wrists, flooding my senses. And I could hear nothing but our breaths, gradually slowing and becoming perfectly synchronised. I didn't know a first kiss could feel like this.

When we parted, the sweet taste of his lips lingered on mine. He took a step backward onto the front path with an expression of pleasant bewilderment. He blew upwards to move some hair that was covering his eyes.

'Wow. That was really something,' he breathed. 'I hope to see you next week.'

'I bet you say that to all the girls,' I returned with a cheeky, yet affectionate, smile.

As I closed the door, I saw his eyebrows raise as if he were about to say something. Leave them wanting more, that's what I always say.

I leant back on the door, giggling like a giddy teenager. It didn't matter that I'd just shared a passionate kiss with a prostitute. I felt alive.

I ran to my bed and flopped down onto the covers, touching my fingers up to my mouth, just to make sure it had been real. I felt my phone vibrate, and reached around trying to find it among the pillows. It was Emily. Of course she wanted to know how my first kiss in ten years had gone. She had no patience. When I answered, Emily was breathless and frantic.

'God girl, don't you answer your phone?' She was very loud for this time on a Monday morning. 'I've been trying to reach you for half an hour!'

'Okay, calm down,' I said. 'I'm here. What's up?'

'I'm so sorry. I didn't find out until nine this morning that your prostitute has laryngitis and isn't able to make it,' said Emily. 'I didn't want you to be sitting around all morning on your day off waiting for a man. That thought was just too depressing.'

I was silent.

'Are you disappointed?' Emily sighed, 'I'm so sorry. I'll make it up to you. I'll come over tonight with a cake and a card.'

The card! I left my phone on the bed and ran to where I'd thrown the card in the hallway.

I slowly bent down and picked it up. At the time I'd thrown it, I hadn't paid attention, but now looking closely, the envelope had my full name and address printed on the front. This was obviously unusual for a birthday card. Still confused, I tore it open. Out fell a credit card. Shiny and new. I felt my jaw drop.

I ran down the hallway and threw the door open, looking around wildly with just enough time to see a motorbike with fluorescent markings, laden with packages, pull out of the cul-de-sac.

I'd passionately kissed the postman.

'Emily,' I yelled towards the bedroom. 'I'm going to have to call you back.'

TO TAKE A LOVER

kellie m cox

The roll of the 'r' off his tongue caught Ruby's attention across the busy beachside café. An attractive stranger with strands of messy hair responded passionately to the unheard voice at the end of the phone. The smell of the fresh coffee brew lingered through the shopfront. The scent familiar from hours of waiting tables, day after long day, unlikely the explanation for the visceral reaction she felt to the scene around her.

Moving towards the handsome stranger, she detected words spoken in the language of love, a language rarely heard in this part of the coast. She arrived by his side as he placed his phone on the table. Handing the menu over, her fingers lingered momentarily as they held the bound pages between them. In the short pause, he looked up at her, his green eyes piercing into hers.

'*Bonjour*,' he greeted her.

'Hello,' Ruby replied, her brash Australian accent in contrast to the beautiful sounds his mouth formed with a single word.

'I mean *bonjour* as well.' Her voice caught as she fumbled to add the suitable greeting of reply. 'I'm Ruby and I'll be serving you today. Can I get you a coffee as you look over the menu?'

'*Oui, un café s'il vous plaît.*'

'Excuse me?'

'Oh, yes, a coffee please.'

'Okay.' Ruby turned from the stranger. Her legs felt heavy, as if walking through a dream as she weaved through the small circular tables that housed their morning guests. Her stomach reacted to the aromas of the breakfast meals around her, the freshly toasted bread, the sizzling bacon, and frying eggs blended in harmony. She handed the order to the tall barista behind the counter who looked down in readiness for his next instruction.

'What type of coffee. You've just written coffee?'

'I don't know,' Ruby replied.

'What type of milk, full cream, soy, almond, coconut?'

'I don't know.'

'Ruby, no one drinks a normal coffee anymore. Go back and get the order right.'

'I can't.'

The barista scoffed. An obvious sign of both disinterest and frustration at the young waiter.

'Well, I'm not making another if you've got it wrong. You can come back here and do it yourself. Hear me?'

'Yep,' Ruby replied, half-heartedly as she had nothing more to say. Only one half of her had returned to the counter. The other half, the most important part of her, was still standing at the table mesmerised by the striking green eyes of the handsome stranger.

After her busy breakfast shift all Ruby wanted to do was to dive under the cool salty waters of her favourite beach. She walked over the grassy hill that led to the secret inlet, her favourite spot away from tourists when she noticed a large striped towel in the position she would normally lay to tan after her ocean swim. She moved closer to the spot to discover a book left open, face down on the cloth. A book of poems, an unusual read for a tourist. She grimaced seeing the crinkled spine stretched flat. It was disappointing when people didn't look after their books and creased the spine or worse, dog-eared the pages. There was a lot to understand about a person by the way they cared for their precious paperbacks.

Ruby found a spot and placed her own towel down on the soft sand. She anchored one of the corners with a beach bag and the other with her thongs. Pulling her floral sundress over her head, she released her long auburn hair from its tightly held bun. She strode towards the glistening water in front of her, anticipating that first sensual dive under the clear waters. As she reached the shoreline, she noticed a hand waving in the air, the international sign for distress in the water. Someone was in trouble in the crashing waves. Quickening her step she rushed into the water, diving under to gather speed against the strong pull of the waters towards land.

She swam quickly to the hapless tourist, unfamiliar with the dangerous conditions of the Queensland surf. As she reached him his head sank under the water. She pulled him to the surface and turned him onto his back, speaking words of support to calm him.

'You're okay,' she reassured him. 'Let's get you back to the sand.'

He followed her lead as she supported his torso and swam with him to shore. She had two choices to make, swim the short distance to the large boulders, which would require him climbing over them to get to safety, or take the fastest route to shallower waters where they could ground their feet on the wet sand and walk as much as possible.

The man was quiet on the return swim, likely saving his precious oxygen levels until they returned to normal. Unsure of how much water he had swallowed, Ruby didn't pressure him for words, instead waiting until they got to safety to assess his condition.

They reached the shallows, and she encouraged him to find his feet. She held him as they walked towards the beach and when they were safe in ankle deep water, she allowed him to collapse onto the sand. He looked down and took deep breaths until the panic subsided. Ruby searched the area for any assistance, but the quiet beach was empty. She fell to her knees to speak to him. He swept his long wavy hair from his face and looked back at her. His green eyes once more caught her attention. She held her breath for a minute as she prepared for him to speak. The realisation hit her that she had just rescued the handsome stranger she had served breakfast to hours earlier.

'*Merci*,' he began in his native language before moving to English. 'I mean thank you, thank you so very much. You saved my life.' He stopped as he began to recognise the face before him. 'I met you in the café.'

Ruby smiled. 'Yes, you did.' She paused. 'But you're okay now, you probably would have just drifted around the headland and been saved by lifeguards. That's really where you should be swimming, between the flags, not out here.'

'I didn't know. The water, it's so calm.'

'The ocean here is beautiful but deadly,' she replied. 'Everything in Australia wants to kill you. Even our crystal blue sea.'

He smiled a wide toothy smile at her, and her mouth followed with an open grin. He raised his hand to move a strand of her long locks that were plastered against her face. He tucked the strand of wayward hair behind her ear.

'You are my beautiful guardian angel.'

She placed her hand over his on her face and melted into his masculine fingers.

'I'm Ruby.'

'I'm Sebastian,' he replied with the most delicious of accents she had ever heard.

'May I kiss you?'

Shocked by the sudden request but caught up in the romance of the magical moment, she simply nodded her head.

His lips met hers with a gentle touch. He tasted salty and sweet at the same time. He moved his lips apart to take her in. She closed her eyes and allowed her body to find his firm chest. He stroked the side of her face. They stayed enmeshed together for what felt like a dream, an eternity. It was the most sensual scene Ruby could ever imagine, far more than any poetic prose she had so far managed to write.

When their lips separated, Ruby felt overwhelmingly alone, as if a part of her she didn't even know existed, had been ripped from her.

'Would you come with me to my room?' Sebastian asked in hushed tones.

'Yes.' Ruby didn't hesitate.

Time stopped and the rest of the afternoon was spent lying naked between fresh white sheets. When they did move from the bed, they took in the view from the balcony overlooking the ocean that had brought the two lovers together. They shared their laughter and conversation as easily as they had shared their first kiss. The similarities between them were incredible. Both lovers of the written word, Sebastian a reader of poetry, Ruby an avid writer of prose. They discussed music, the arts, their dreams and hopes for their futures.

It was as if they were destined to meet, to fall madly in love and never again part. Sebastian lamented over his disappointment at not yet having children and the imagined joy at raising a family full of kids.

Ruby visualised the gorgeous man in front of her as the father of her own children. A masculine protective, but gentle and loving figure in their lives. She watched him speak about his dreams and his life in his home in Paris and she yearned with every part of her body for him to invite her to return home with him. Every romance novel she had ever read would pale in comparison to the beautiful life she would share with this gorgeous French man.

'Why have you never married and have kids?' It was obvious this man was capable of great love, and Ruby couldn't imagine why he had not been secured already by a local beauty.

'I am married.' Sebastian replied. 'To Fanny.'

Ruby jumped from the bed. 'You're what? Married. Not like separated, but married?'

'*Oui,*' he replied.

'Then what are you doing here with me? Why did you ask me to come back to your room?'

'My wife, she understands.'

'What?' Ruby's voice raised in volume as she gathered her strewn clothing from the other side of the room.

'My wife, she does not care much for this,' Sebastian glanced around the room, arm outstretched indicating the messy bed and half eaten room service. 'She has an extraordinary career and is busy with her own life.'

'That doesn't make it okay to screw random women you meet at the beach.'

Sebastian moved from the bed to find Ruby half-dressed. He reached out and took her hands into his. 'We made love my darling. And it is okay. I am permitted to take a lover.'

'Well, it's not okay by me.' Ruby shook her hands free. 'It's deceitful. I thought this was the beginning of something special.'

'It is Ruby ... it is.'

'Not for me, buddy. No way mate.' Her thick Australian accent returning to empathise her distain at the unfolding situation.

'Please Ruby, listen. I want you to meet Fanny. Meet her and you will see she is perfectly fine with this. She has her life and I have mine.'

'That's just bizarre and I'm not into it. Whatever this dirty little arrangement the two of you have, it's not for me. Why don't you just get divorced if you're not happy together?'

'I love her, and I would never do that to her.'

'You love her?' The hurtful words tugged at Ruby's stomach causing the same visceral reaction felt just hours earlier on seeing Sebastian for the first time.

'Yes, but I believe we can love two people at once.'

Ruby listened to several days of incessant pleading from Sebastian before she finally agreed to meet his much-loved wife. Fanny had been in Sydney presenting a TED talk when Ruby had spent the day with Sebastian. She now returned to the seaside tourist town for a few days of rest and relaxation before the couple were to fly home to Paris together. Ruby was conflicted. She wanted to like the woman Sebastian had promised his life too. Yet she also held a deep yearning to despise everything about her.

She decided to meet the couple, and hoped they would prove to have a relationship that made sense for all the right reasons. It might provide some comfort to Ruby, an explanation of why she and Sebastian could never be. At the same time it could offer hope that one day she would meet the perfect person too.

Ruby dressed in a little black dress and heels, the perfect combination for any occasion. She entered the busy restaurant to see the most stunning woman ever created. Fanny was sitting at the bar, slim legs crossed at the knee, her short blonde bob falling perfectly against an elongated neck, her style effortlessly coming together as if she was born to be beautiful. Sebastian sat across from her, his back to the door. He leant in and laughed, his hand on Fanny's knee as they shared a joke just for two.

Ruby froze, the fear response forced her to stand and witness the scene before her brain could catch up and allow her to turn and run back out to the street. Fanny caught the eyes of the local woman and jumped to her feet to greet her. Sebastian turned to watch his wife, but remained seated, a wide smile plastered on his face. Fanny strode towards Ruby, her long lean legs consuming every piece of earth they traversed. She reached Ruby and wrapped her arms around the terrified woman. She placed her lips on one cheek and brushed the sensitive skin. Slowly she lifted her head, turning it to land a delicate kiss on the other cheek. She placed both soft hands on Ruby's upper arms, the contact sending goosebumps across her skin. Her stomach cramped. What was it with the French? They seemed to have such an effect on her.

Fanny finally spoke, 'You are more beautiful than Sebastian could even describe. I can see why he has fallen for you.'

'You are stunning.' Was all Ruby could reply. Her brain could not catch up to the instinctive reactions her body and mind were having in response to the woman.

'*Merci*, such a compliment from a natural beauty such as yourself. Come join us for a drink before we share a meal.'

Fanny ushered Ruby to the bar. Sebastian stood on her arrival and greeted her with a kiss on the lips. She was sure Fanny's smile widened even further on seeing their embrace.

'This feels really strange,' Ruby said.

'Not for us,' Fanny replied. 'We French have a different way of looking at love and intimacy. We know that attraction can be found in multiple places, and we embrace it. In fact, I wish I had met you before Sebastian did.'

Sebastian spoke up. 'Fanny, that may be, how do you say, a little too much for Ruby.'

'Nonsense,' Fanny replied taking Ruby's hand into hers. She pushed their palms together and entwined her fingers between Ruby's. 'I can see Ruby feels something too.'

The dinner conversation was tantalising with both Fanny and Sebastian sharing the details of their own love story including how they met. Ruby shared her version of rescuing the handsome Sebastian from the waves of her favourite beach. As the end of the night approached, none of the trio quite knew how to say goodbye. It would be natural to assume Fanny and Sebastian would retire to their hotel room, but

Ruby felt unsure where she wanted to go. As complicated as it was to be around the couple, she also knew she didn't want to go home alone to her tired single room unit. She became painfully aware of how lonely her life was. Before she had time to suggest anything, Sebastian kissed Ruby good night and offered to see her to her car.

Once home, Ruby tossed and turned in the queen-sized bed that now felt far too large for just one. When she tried to close her eyes, she pictured the dishevelled French couple, legs entangled, sensual mouths exploring each other's bodies. Sleep would not come easily this night.

The following morning, Ruby called Sebastian. As much as she knew she should just forget the visiting couple, she was already involved. It had come on as quickly as the legendary arrow shot straight from cupid's bow. There was no way to contain the eruption of emotions that flowed from her soul for the very first time. She skipped to the beach to meet the pair. She had two days before they would disappear from her life, and she needed to see this through. Ruby would not hesitate, for feelings like these came once in a lifetime.

Sebastian and Fanny arrived moments later. As towels were pushed together to form a large blanket of protection from the white sand, the trio found their spots and looked with anticipation from one to the other.

'We have some news,' Sebastian announced. 'We spent all night talking and realised we want different things from life. Fanny wants to stay on and tour further with her speaking engagements. I'm going to return home to Paris.'

Ruby was shocked. She had imagined a completely different night for the lovers, one in which their passion for each other was reignited after the sexually charged dinner date. Sebastian began to speak once more.

'And Ruby, I would like it very much if you would come home to Paris with me.'

Ruby was stunned into silence. Words failed and her brain struggled to make sense of what she was hearing. She turned to try to read the emotion in Fanny's expression.

Fanny placed both hands on Ruby's bare legs. She leant forward, a warm smile on her face. 'You must Ruby. Sebastian can do nothing but speak of you and the life he wants. You can give him everything I do not desire. A wife and family, children to fulfil his deepest desire to be a father. You have my every blessing to go to Paris. I will stay on here. You will never have to think of me again. Just go and make him happy … for me.'

Ruby edged forward on the towel towards Fanny. She placed both hands on her face, just as Sebastian had done to her days earlier. 'May I?' She sought Fanny's consent.

Fanny nodded, closed her eyes, parted her mouth, and welcomed the soft lips to hers. Ruby drank in the taste of the woman, she let her hands hold the soft skin and her mind focused on utilising every sense. She breathed in the delicate floral fragrances of her freshly showered flesh, she listened intently to the purr that rose from her throat. The moment lasted forever and when the kiss finished, she dropped both hands to find Fanny's and leant down to speak.

'I want to come with you to Sydney. Do you possibly feel the same?'

Fanny's face erupted, she threw her arms around Ruby and held her in a tight embrace. When it ended, the women's hands locked together, and they looked towards Sebastian.

'I'm sorry Sebastian,' Ruby said tentatively.

Sebastian's head dropped; his arms fell limp at his side. He sighed a deep sorrowful exhale before finally being able to respond, 'I understand.'

'I fell in love with two people at once,' Ruby added.

'When a heart is capable of loving, it wants to be filled with great love. I can see that in the two of you,' Sebastian answered.

The trio enjoyed the rest of the day at the beach, grateful to have found and felt great love and aware that intimate love between two will ebb and flow but a grand love, it must be honoured. Sebastian caught an earlier flight the next day to return to his life in Paris. The women promised to visit often.

'Fanny, Fanny, they're here. I can see them parking. Oh, the girls have gotten so big in just a few months,' Ruby yelled out to her wife.

'I don't know how they're all going to fit in. Maybe we should've let them get a hotel.'

'We'll squash in together and make it work.'

Fanny and Ruby looked down to the street to see Sebastian, his wife, Nicola and their three young girls hold hands as they crossed the busy Bondi Beach intersection. The apartment, although small would house the visitors for the girls' first ever summer Christmas.

The women held the door ajar excited to greet their goddaughters. The elevator doors opened, and the three young girls ran into familiar arms. 'Aunty Fanny, Aunty Ruby, can we go to the beach now?'

'Let's give your Mama and Papa time to unpack. It is a long flight, and they might want to rest first,' Fanny replied to the excited sisters.

'*Non*,' the youngest of the girls yelled back in reply. 'Beach now!'

'That's not very polite young lady.' Nicola chastised her daughter.

'How about Fanny and I take the girls to the beach, and you and Sebastian can get settled in.' Ruby suggested. 'Have a rest, grab something to eat, take your time and we'll meet you over there,'

Nicola sighed as she embraced Ruby. '*Merci*, that would be lovely.'

Sebastian hugged Ruby tightly and turned to his daughters. 'That's probably a good idea. Your Aunty Ruby is a much better swimmer than your Pappa. Did you know she once saved my life? I nearly drowned in the waves, and she swam out to rescue me.'

'I saved your life and then you saved mine. That's what family do for each other.' Ruby hugged the only man she would ever love. She held him for the longest time, for he introduced her to the reality of a grand love.

Her life was far richer than she ever imagined it could be, because of him.

A GOOD MAN

christine betts

'Is my friend okay?' Dani spoke to the top of the doctor's head.

'Mmm,' he said, eyes trained on the underside of her foot.

'You're lucky it wasn't worse.' He ignored her question but spoke softly as he dug around in her flesh for shards of glass. 'Shouldn't have taken your shoes off,' he said.

No kidding?

He pulled one bloodied sliver of glass out, then another, and dropped them into a metal dish. There was no pain, just some tugging at her skin. The pain would come once the anaesthetic wore off, and the hangover and shame set in. The doctor applied a dressing, then wrapped her foot in a soft bandage.

'Keep it clean and dry. The nurse will give you some paracetamol. If the site gets infected, go to your G.P.' He pointed at her fabulous bright-blue high-heeled shoes. 'Might be best to leave those off.'

The heat rose in Dani's face, but she clenched her teeth to stop her from saying something she might regret. He tossed his latex gloves in the bin, turned to his computer, and tapped out something. His hands were smooth and pale, nothing like those of the itinerant fruit pickers, surfers, and backpackers she patched up during her shifts at the clinic in town. She lifted her eyes and stared at his profile. He gave his full attention to the screen.

He doesn't remember me ...

To him, she was just another drunken idiot who'd found themselves in the E.D. in the middle of the night. To her, now, he was just a mansplaining tool. *Doctor bloody Perfect with his perfect hair and perfect smile.* She had no idea how she could have found him attractive all those years ago.

Dani grabbed her bag and rifled through its contents. Where was her phone? She slumped back into the seat. Her mum was right. She had to stop hanging out with her old school friends, especially Caroline.

She stood and tried her weight on the dodgy foot. Dr Perfect continued to type, and she was suddenly embarrassed at her awkward hanging around. Obviously, he had signed off on their interaction. She grabbed her shoes and stuffed them in her bag. If she'd listened to her mum about the shoes, about going out with her old schoolmates, about drinking too much, she wouldn't be in this mess.

'Thanks,' she said and headed for the door.

'You don't remember me, do you?' he said to her back.

She stopped but didn't look at him, busying herself with patting her pockets in search of the lost phone. She hoped her voice wouldn't betray her.

'Should I?' She shrugged as though she had sufficiently answered his question.

He said nothing. A nurse knocked on the open door; Angela was another old school buddy and now one of the school mums. Dr Perfect's attention stayed glued to the computer screen. Dani followed Angela into the corridor.

'I missed a big night, eh? Caroline's okay. Two broken fingers,' she said. She gestured at Dani's foot. 'You need crutches?'

'No.' Dani demonstrated by standing on the damaged foot. 'Without the chunks of glass in it, it's just a regular foot again.'

'Amazing,' Angela whispered, a hint of a smile on her lips. 'Don't be a hero. I know it's hard for you doctors to be the patient for a change.'

'I'm fine,' Dani said.

Angela nodded ever so slightly at Dr Perfect. 'He's a bit of all right,' she murmured.

Dani rolled her eyes.

He's all yours.

Angela laughed. 'Oh, by the way, your *boyfriend* is waiting out front.'

'You know I don't have a boyfriend,' Dani said.

Angela winked. 'Have fun.'

Dani hit the 'exit' button and hobbled out through the automatic doors. The waiting room was empty but for an elderly couple at the Triage window and a man crouched on the floor on the far wall, his phone charger plugged into a socket. Her high school bestie, Timbo Johnson. He was definitely not her boyfriend. She had been aware of his presence all night, on the fringe of their messy, drunken group.

They'd been friends all those years ago, but he'd gone off to chase stardom and never looked back.

'Hey, Timbo.'

He startled at the sound of her voice and jumped up, brushing his jeans. His long dark hair, that earlier had been pulled back into a ponytail, draped over his face. He held out his phone. The shattered screen glinted in the bright lights of the waiting room.

'It's dead.'

He pulled the charger out of the wall, coiled it round his hand and slid it into his pocket then turned to look at her, one side of his face swollen and bruised.

Dani gasped. 'What happened to you?'

'Caroline smacked me a couple of times. That's how it all started. She picked a fight with that raucous hen's night group, and it was on.' His voice carried a twang of accent.

'So, that was you who carried her out over your shoulder?'

He nodded and lowered his voice. 'Someone had to. Cops asked if I wanted to press charges.'

They grinned at each other.

'It's great to see you,' he said.

'You were avoiding me at the pub,' Dani said playfully.

He shook his head.

'I wanted to say hi, but you were with the hockey girls.' He shrugged. 'It was all very chaotic.'

Dani laughed softly. 'Oh yes, the old hockey girls ... Always a lot of fun. I've missed you, Timbo,' she said.

He held his arms out for a hug. She slotted hers around his waist and rested her head on his chest. He smelt of other people's cigarettes, sweat and the remnants of his cologne, warm and spicy. He pulled back and looked into her eyes.

'Timbo? What?' Dani laughed.

He squeezed her shoulders lightly and let go. 'Most people just call me Tim these days. You look so different.'

She laughed. The long blonde braids she'd worn as a teenager were gone. Her hair was cropped and pink, and piercings ran the length of her ears.

'So do you. Loved the ponytail earlier.'

He ran his fingers through his tangled mane. 'It's all the rage in Nashville.'

'Oooh, you're so fancy,' she said.

He laughed and shook his head shyly. He'd obviously not hit the big time with his music career, or she would have heard about it. His mum would have been talking about it all over town. Dani's mum did when she'd gotten into medical school.

'Hey, let's go to Barney's,' she said.

'I can't believe that dump is still there. When I flew in yesterday, I got mum to drive down the esplanade on the way home.'

'When I flew in,' she mocked.

They both laughed and wandered out into the warm night. There were no taxis at the rank. The few in town would be busy with revellers from the pubs and clubs on the esplanade. Dani searched her bag again.

'Can't call an Uber. I've lost my phone,' she said. Her foot throbbed, and she had lost her denim jacket, but she wasn't ready for the night to end. It was just getting good. 'I can walk.'

'I can always throw you over my shoulder,' he said.

'My foot's fine. Merely a flesh wound.'

'I'm sorry about tonight,' he said. 'I don't know why Caroline wants to fight when she's drunk.'

'God, it wasn't your fault. Caro might have a husband and two kids, but she hasn't changed a bit since school,' Dani said.

'You remember that school dance?' Tim said.

'When she drank half a bottle of vodka?' Dani replied. 'I think she might have a drinking problem.'

'Don't we all?' he said.

She glanced at him, and he smiled. 'Sober five years.'

'That's great,' Dani said.

Tim held out his arm for her and she glanced up at him and smiled. She slipped her hand into the crook of his elbow. He squeezed it lightly and Dani leant against him for a moment. *I've missed you*, she wanted to say but didn't.

They took the path that led from the hospital past the strip of motels leading into town and up onto the esplanade. A few hardy souls with fishing rods mingled with the partying holiday makers on the footpath in front of Barney's All Night Bakery and the smells of baked goods and sea salt hung in the night air. They joined the queue.

'How's life been? Mum said you're a doctor,' he said.

'Your intel is correct. I am a doctor, but I still live with my mum and I'm shoeless in a twenty-four-hour bakery.'

'Mum said you have a son.'

Dani smiled. 'Eliot. He's twelve. But that's enough about me. So, you're back? Like forever?' They shuffled forward in the line, closer to the golden pies and sausage rolls.

He nodded. 'No doubt you've heard the rumours that as of yesterday, I'm back in my childhood bedroom. I'm the new music teacher at the high school. You know what they say, those who can, do, those who can't, teach …'

'That's bullshit. Teachers are the most undervalued people in the world. Don't start with that kind of attitude.'

'Next please,' the man behind the counter bellowed. They had erected heavy plastic screens during the pandemic and never taken them down.

'Two sausage rolls and a pastie, please,' Dani said. She turned to Tim. 'What are you having?'

He laughed. 'Same,' he said to the server.

'And six sauces,' Dani added.

'I got it,' Tim said.

He pulled out his wallet, but Dani shook her head. 'I can't let the failed muso pay for his own welcome-home meal.'

'I don't care who pays for it, just cough up and get out of the way,' the server said.

Dani waved her card over the EFTPOS machine. They grabbed their bundles of white paper bags and headed across the road to a bench beside the concrete skate bowl. The rising sun was a smudge on the horizon. It would be another scorcher weekend to end the school holidays.

Dani's foot throbbed and her head was about to join in the fun. She wished she had bought a Coke. Her mouth flooded with saliva as she squirted tomato sauce on the pastie.

'Hey, remember that time in grade eight when we were playing dodge ball?'

He groaned. 'I can't believe you brought that up.'

'Ooh,' she said, laughing. 'How could I not? You ended up sitting right on top of me. Like straddling me.'

He glared at her for a moment, then laughed. 'Yeah, that's still up there with my worst high school moments,' he said. 'Actually, I've had only a couple of more mortifying moments in my life.'

'If sitting on me is one of the worst things that's happened to you, you've been very lucky.'

She stared at her pastie.

'You okay,' he said.

She shrugged. 'I was just condescended to for half an hour by the guy who knocked me up and bailed thirteen years ago,' she said, and took a huge bite.

Tim stared at her. He looked back towards the distant hospital. She waited for his brain to catch up.

'Who? The doctor?'

She nodded, took another bite, and chewed.

'Are you sure?'

She nodded more emphatically, swallowed, and laughed. 'It's not something you tend to forget.'

'That's the guy who made you drop out of medical school?'

'You heard about that all the way over in Nashville?' She sighed. 'I went back, though. A couple of years later.'

'You haven't seen him since?'

She shook her head. 'Til tonight.'

'Fark,' Tim said, years of living in the States clear in his accent. 'Tonight ... Did he ...?'

'What? Beg for forgiveness?' She shook her head and stared into her pastie. 'I pretended I didn't remember him.'

Tim dropped his sausage roll, put his arm around her shoulder, and squeezed. 'If he let you go, then he was a dick. And now he's Dr Dick.'

Dani laughed, head back, mouth open. 'His name is Richard.' She snorted. 'He's so prim and proper and there I was with my stripper heels and shards of beer bottle glass in my foot, and oh *my God*, I was *so* drunk.' She pulled away from Tim and bit into her pastie.

Headlights illuminated them, the trees, the skate bowl, as a car swung around the corner and pulled up in the parking lot.

'Danielle?'

They both turned as the doctor's face appeared over the top of the car. Dani turned back to the sunrise.

'A black Audi. So original,' she mumbled.

'I knew it was you. You look so different ...' He smiled and gestured at himself. 'I thought you'd remember me.'

'Oh, I remember you, Richard. Happy? Now go away,' Dani said. The car beeped and flashed as he locked it and walked around in front of her.

'The lady wants to be left alone,' Tim said.

'It's okay. I got this,' Dani said.

He looked into her eyes. 'Have you got this?'

She nodded.

'I'll be right there if you need me.' He pointed at the railing overlooking the beach. He took his sausage rolls and sat on the concrete, looking out to sea. Dani smiled. All through school, he had been there for her. She probably wouldn't have even made it to uni if it wasn't for his encouragement.

'Danielle?'

She took a deep breath and turned back to Richard. He walked slowly, as though she were a wild animal, and he didn't want to startle her. He was about two metres away.

'What are you doing here?' she said.

'Angela, the nurse ... She said you might be here.' He held up her phone. 'It was under the desk in the exam room.'

He leant forward and offered it to her. She put her hand out and he took a step towards her, looked her in the eye, and placed it on her upturned palm.

'Thanks.' She tapped the screen. The battery was dead.

'I meant, what are you doing here? Here.' She waved her hand towards the town she had grown up in. He stared at her for a moment, then shook his head.

'Travelling north. My, ahh, marriage just broke up and I've got a job offer in Cairns. Been working my way up the coast. Just completed a week's locum. I leave tomorrow. Did you qualify?'

She nodded. 'I'm a G.P. at the clinic here in town.'

He shook his head slowly. 'You wanted to be a surgeon.'

She pursed her lips and narrowed her eyes. He stopped, perhaps noticing Dani's arched eyebrow, warning him to proceed carefully.

'Can I take you to breakfast? I'd love to catch up, see what you've been up to all these years.'

Dani looked down at the remains of the pastie in her hand. 'I've got breakfast covered, thanks. And lunch.' She gestured at the bags in her lap.

He smiled. 'Okay. I get it, you're still mad. After all these years, I was hoping we could be friends.' He took a step backwards.

Dani shook her head. 'I've got all the friends I need here.'

'Oh yes, you've got friends who get pissed and pick fights in pubs. Nice.'

'Just go, Richard. Get in your car and go to Cairns.'

He took two paces towards the Audi and stopped.

'Gladly,' he said. 'You're obviously not the same disciplined, hard-working girl I knew then, anyway.'

'You don't know a thing about me. No, I'm not the same girl I was. I'm a woman and a G.P. and a fucking pillar of the community, so get in your Audi and piss off.'

He barked out a laugh.

'Nice. Real nice.' He shook his head and stalked back to the car. He didn't meet her eye as she watched him reverse out and drive away. Last time she had sobbed and begged, and he hadn't looked at her then either.

The rising sun sat halfway between the sea and the sky, a red glow in an otherwise grey world. Tim turned to her.

'You okay?'

Dani shrugged.

'Can I walk you home? You still live on Ocean Street?'

Her foot throbbed, and she wobbled a little as she stood.

'Let me piggyback you.' He turned around.

She put her hands on his shoulders, and he launched her up onto his back.

'It's only fair I get to straddle you this time,' she said.

He didn't respond. They walked slowly along the footpath to where it met the road.

'You didn't tell him about his son?'

They crossed the road in silence and turned into the laneway she had lived in all her life. The only home her son had ever known. The patio light was on, her mother's beloved succulents filling every available space in the small front yard. Tim crouched and let her down gently.

'Eliot is my son. Richard doesn't deserve to know about my son.'

'Doesn't he deserve the opportunity to do the right thing?'

'No, Tim.' She put her hands on her hips. 'Richard had that opportunity and he blew it. He didn't even ask. I suppose he assumed I'd used the money he threw at me that day. I mean, I used it to buy baby stuff, but that's not what he intended me to use it for.' She looked up at him, challenging him to disagree with her.

He didn't.

'Good night,' she said and hobbled towards the stairs.

'Dani. I'm sorry. I'm a klutz. I shouldn't have said what I said.'

She turned back.

'How could you take his side? Bloody men ...'

He took a step towards her, hands up in surrender. 'I know. We're all dreadful.'

She couldn't help herself; she laughed. 'Present company excluded. You were always one of the good ones. Even when we were playing dodgeball.'

They both laughed softly.

'Thanks for the lift home,' she said.

'You're welcome. Good night.' He gestured at the pale blue sky above them.

'Shit.' She puffed a stray hair out of her eyes. 'Eliot has soccer in a couple of hours. It's gonna be a long day.' She dug around in her bag for her keys.

'Can I take you out for dinner tonight?' Tim said.

She looked up at him, head cocked to one side. 'Timbo Johnson, are you asking me out on a date?'

He laughed. 'Indeed, I am. Your son, too, if you want. Hell, your mum can come, if it means I get to spend more time with you.'

Tingles ran up her spine. She smiled at him. 'How about just me tonight.'

A magpie started up its morning song, high up in the pine tree across the road. Tim reached out and took Dani's hand. She looked down at his calloused hand as he entwined his fingers with hers.

'Your hands are so rough,' she murmured. 'Sorry, just an observation.' She thought back to Richard's soft, pale hands. Dr Perfect had a pretty face, but beyond that, she wasn't sure what she had ever seen in him.

Tim turned his hand over.

'Guitar strings are brutal. The callouses help.'

She laughed softly. 'Yes, a hard shell can be very useful.'

He looked into her eyes. 'Seriously, Dani, tonight? Just you would be perfect,' he said and leant down to kiss her.

'Hey, don't get ahead of yourself, mate. You don't get to first base before the date.'

He laughed. 'Dani, I should have asked you out years ago.'

'I would have said no.'

His face fell.

'I *would* have said no ...'

He laughed. 'And now?'

She pulled him towards her, winding her hands around his waist and kissed him, a smile on both their lips.

'*Now*, I'd say yes, because now I know a good man when he lands in my lap.'

OLD LYNG SINCE

selena jane

The make-up artist took the stemmed glass from Rose's hand and spun her around in the chair to face her. Scrutinising Rose's face, she nodded.

'I can't take all the credit, you were already a stunner.'

Squirming under her intensity, Rose focussed on the girl's nose ring.

'Can I go then?'

'Go for it. I mixed a bit of sunscreen into your foundation.'

'Thank you,' Rose murmured.

Not bothering to check the artist's work, Rose crossed the hotel room towards the bedroom, slipped off her robe and stepped into the pale pink silk dress laid out for her on the bed. The other bridesmaids' giddy conversation about their fortunate pairings carried to her from the balcony. A groan escaped the back of Rose's throat. Angus Rory was to be her partner today, and the mere sound of his name made the bile rise at the back of her throat. She sat on the bed and fastened her sandals, careful to lean over at just the right angle so as not to disturb her hair piled on top of her head.

Angus Rory, a Scottish braggart.

Rose had endured a whole day of him as they'd toured Edinburgh Castle when she was fourteen. According to Angus Rory, Scotland, and everything about Scotland, from its castles to moorlands to coastline, was far superior to her native England. She'd been so naïve back then; everyone had warned her.

The bride to be, her cousin Melanie, waved to her from the balcony. Rose pushed her irritation towards her cousin deep down. Today was not the day to hold petty grudges. She'd pleaded with Melanie to allow her to change partners, but she was adamant that for height reasons, Angus was Rose's best match. Melanie had conveniently overlooked the fact she herself was twice the size of her husband to be. Rose straightened her back and took a deep breath. All would be well, as her dear grandmother would say. This time, she would be prepared for Angus.

One by one, she ticked off her curled fingers in her lap. Firstly, she was no longer that pimply teenager with glasses whose witty responses didn't make it to the surface, like when he'd told her she resembled Velma from *Scooby-Doo*. Rose had wanted to tell him he looked like Shaggy with his scrappy excuse for a beard. She unfurled another finger. Secondly, today he would wear a kilt, not a smart dress kilt, but an old moth ball ancestry hand-me-down, and she'd decided that alone would give her loads of mileage. Rose smiled and nodded. Thirdly, she pulled back another finger and looked up, frowning. Well, she couldn't think of a third, but was sure once she laid eyes on him again, she'd find something to challenge him on.

She stood, smoothed the folds of her silk dress, and walked out onto the balcony.

'Rose,' the girls squealed in unison, wobbling towards her like magnets.

'She's so pale, like a pretty vampire.' One giggled, reaching out to touch her.

Rose's eyes scanned their tanned shoulders and faltered. Maybe she should have taken her mother's advice and had that spray tan.

'She's just like that girl from *Twilight*,' another slurred.

They twittered on as if she weren't there. She'd heard Australians could hold their liquor, but not their tongues. She could shut them down with a witty remark, but for the sake of her cousin, she pressed her lips together and smiled.

Her sister Lily slipped her arm through hers and whispered in her ear, 'Rose, I think the pink looks beautiful against your pale skin.'

They locked eyes, silent words passing between the two sisters.

Melanie pressed a glass of champagne into her hand and rolled her eyes.

'You've got some catching up to do.'

Rose nodded, her thoughts returning to Angus Rory. She'd heard his plane had been delayed; with any luck, he'd miss the wedding. She looked out over Sydney harbour, taking in the sights of the Opera House gleaming like an igloo, the majestic Harbour Bridge, boats of all shapes and sizes, the green and yellow ferries, the seagulls, all covered in sparkling sunshine. No, she would not allow Angus Rory to ruin her Australian trip.

The car door swung open, and Rose's white calf slipped from the limousine, anchoring her pink sandal on the gravel leading to the church. She fell in behind her cousin's pillows of white fabric.

'My train,' Melanie hissed.

Rose bobbed down to a crouch to straighten Melanie's train. The heat from the gravel hit her face, and she felt her makeup melt. Sweat pooled in her armpits as the sun beat down on her back. A shadow fell over her, blocking the sunlight and she looked up to the see the silhouette of a man in a kilt. She took the offered hand, and he pulled her to standing, drawing her into his chest. Rose looked up, her breath catching at the back of her throat. Amusement danced in the depths of the man's blue eyes.

'Ah, our sweet Rose, wilting in a wee bit of sunshine.'

'Angus?' she sputtered, her well-rehearsed jibes staying at the back of her throat.

'It is I, lassie.' He laughed, kissing the back of her hand.

She snatched her hand from his. She'd been prepared to despise him, but his deep laughter and handsome face disarmed her. He was taller. She'd expected that, but the broadness of his shoulders intimidated her in a way she had not expected. Rose dug her fingernails into her palms.

'You can't talk. Your face is as red as a beet,' she quipped.

'Indeed, it is.' He roared with laughter. 'Shall we?' He offered her his arm.

'You don't escort me now, that's after,' she scoffed, nodding towards the church. 'In Australia you wait at the front of the church and walk me out.' Her eyes widened. 'Well, go on.'

He offered her a slight bow, rolled his hand before her, and snapped his heels together. His long strawberry blonde hair, scraped into a ponytail, bounced on his back as he strode away.

Melanie turned to her. 'Ready?'

Rose nodded, swallowing over the lump in her throat.

Melanie tilted her head. 'I see by the flush of your cheeks you've been reacquainted with Angus. Handsome, isn't he?'

'And annoying as ever.'

Melanie winked. 'Come on, let's get this show on the road.'

Her sister Lily fell in behind her at the entrance to the church, a tissue in hand dabbing Rose's back.

'We need to get you out of this sun.'

'Don't you start.'

Rose stepped onto the red carpet on cue to the music. She felt the gaze of the congregation on her as she glided, but the eyes that bore into her soul were those of Angus Rory. Her eyes flicked to his. Remembering her promise to tease him, she decided to focus on his girly kilt. Her gaze travelled along his torso, to his tie, across his kilt jacket, past his tweed vest to his plaid, purple, red and black kilt. She lingered a little longer on his black leather sporran covering his manhood, her breath caught in her throat. Her eyes travelled on down to his strong bare knees beneath his kilt, this flashing of flesh sending a shock through her small frame.

The ceremony passed in a blur. Rose, with eyes set forward, dared not look to her left, in case he read her thoughts, which were firmly fixed on what lay beneath Angus Rory's kilt. The bride and groom kissed, the congregation clapped, and Angus came to her side, offering his arm. She slipped her arm through his, drawing in his scent of musky aftershave. He guided her forward.

'Ur not gunna ask what's under ma kilt, lassie?'

'Aren't you bored with that question?' she asked as she felt the blush creep to her cheeks.

'Always happy t' oblige,' he said, folding his kilt between his fingers and lifting the edge.

'Stop it,' she hissed.

She bristled as a memory came flooding back of Angus, hand over heart, boasting about his clan, Clan Montgomery, descended from the Vikings. Teasing her about the commonness of her own clan, Clan Stewart. She moved away from him to position herself for photos outside the church. Taking a long overdue breath, she smiled and played the part of doting bridesmaid.

On their way to the Harbour Bridge for photos, Rose stared out of the limousine window, taking in the waterfront views, and listening to Angus chat to the other bridesmaids in his thick Scottish brogue. Her sister Lily, loyal to a fault, ignored his attempts to engage with her. Rose, eager to escape, clambered out of the limousine. Lily found her standing under the Harbour Bridge, clenching her fists. Lily handed her a glass of champagne and Rose gripped the stem and threw the fizzy liquid down her throat.

'How are you and Angus getting along?' Lily whispered.

'He's insufferable. Thinks he's a real ladies' man.'

They looked to where he stood a few feet away, flirting with the two other bridesmaids whose heads were thrown back in laughter. Rose felt a pinch of jealousy zing in her chest. Two could play at that game. She beckoned one of the groomsmen, tapping the side of her empty glass.

Lily guffawed. 'He hasn't changed then?'

'No, he's as infuriating as ever.'

'Don't worry, you'll only have to walk in and sit with Angus during dinner. You can ditch him when the dancing starts. I have spotted some excellent eye candy.'

'Lily, you've only been separated for three months.'

'Oh Rose, you really are a prude. Life is too short, get out there. I intend to. Trust me, when you are married, that's it,' she said, running her finger across her throat.

'In your case apparently marriage is not "it".'

'Five years married was enough for me.'

Rose took her hand. 'I'm sorry, I don't know what's wrong with me today.'

Lily squeezed her hand. 'It's okay, it's the jetlag.'

They turned to the approaching groomsman, carrying two glasses of champagne. Rose threw back her head and squealed. His puzzled look made Lily laugh.

'What did I say?' he mumbled.

'Nothing,' Rose said. 'It's the champagne. Just stand here.'

She felt Angus's eyes slide over to her, and she leant in closer to the groomsman and touched his sleeve. 'Thank you for the champagne.'

He shrugged, completely unaware of the part he was playing.

The photographer arrived. Pulling and prodding them into position, as he impressed the importance of catching the perfect sunset photos. Angus sauntered over with a bridesmaid on each arm.

'Can all the bridesmaids stand in front of their groomsmen and lean back into your partners please. Pretend you like each other,' said the photographer, igniting polite giggles.

'Rose, tilt your chin up and lean in, will you? You're barely touching.'

Angus's arm wrapped around her waist and pulled her back towards him. She felt his broad chest against her bare shoulders, his suit hot from the glaring sun, and his sporran pressed into her lower back.

'That's right, lean your head on his shoulder.'

Rose tilted her head back against his chest. She realised she'd stopped breathing and pushed a breath through her pursed lips.

Angus bent down and whispered in her ear, 'Calm doon Rose, ye be so stiff ye might snap.'

The photographer snapped his fingers, and his assistant came running. 'Do something before we lose this light,' he hissed.

The assistant handed Rose another glass of champagne. 'It's okay, not everyone is comfortable with photographs. Drink this.'

Rose stepped away from Angus and downed the cool liquid.

'I'll no' bite, ye know. Unless ye want me tae,' he said, chuckling.

She couldn't control the blush creeping to her cheeks and turned away. Her sandal caught on a rock, she stumbled, and Rory caught her arm.

'Get off me, Scooby Doo,' she spat.

He let go of her arm, giving her a puzzled look.

'The light, the light,' the photographer yelled.

Rose registered Melanie's pained face and stepped back into position and leant in against Angus's now stiff and unyielding body.

After what seemed like a million photographs, they walked back to the car. Angus squeezed in next to Rose on the bench seat, his thigh pressing against hers. His kilt riding up, revealing his knees and muscled thighs. He caught her looking and spread his thighs; the sporran falling between his legs, drawing her eyes to his manhood. They didn't speak. When they arrived, he strode from the car into the reception without looking back.

The newlyweds stepped onto the dance floor. Rose watched Melanie's new husband's kilt sway from side to side as he swung his bride around. The DJ asked for the wedding party to join them. The other bridesmaids and their partners sauntered onto the dance floor, leaving Rose sitting alone at the table with Angus.

'I suppose we will need to dance,' he said, standing up.

She nodded. Rose allowed herself to be led. Angus pulled her close to his chest with his arm around her back; he took her hand, and they swayed to the music. He avoided eye contact, staring across the dance floor above her head.

'Lassie, we are being a bit daft, what is it that has ye so tied in knots?'

'Too much champagne,' she said.

He nodded and twirled her around in silence.

He looked down at her. 'Jus' th' champagne?'

She shook her head. 'I suppose not. I can't seem to get past the fifteen-year-old boy that you were.'

'I can assure ye, lassie, that much has changed in th' last ten years, if ye'll give me a chance.'

He swirled her around and pulled her close into his body, and they stood still as the music continued.

'The moment I laid eyes on ye today, Rose Butler, thir was a wee explosion in ma heart. Can a lassie forgive a hormone driven fifteen-year-old laddie who needed a thick ear?'

She stared into his now serious blue eyes, as he took her hand and led her outside onto the patio, closing the door on the loud pump of the music. Her knees gave way. She gulped the fresh air as he pressed a glass of water into her hand.

He cocked his head to the side. 'Too much Australian sun and champagne.'

'And Angus Rory.' She giggled.

'May I kiss you Rose?' He brushed a stray hair behind her ear.

She felt the heat of his gaze upon her lips and nodded.

He leant down and crushed his soft pillowy lips to hers. Never had she experienced such soft flesh on hers, hot and wet. She pushed him back and took a deep breath.

He laughed.

'You, you took my breath away. Literally,' she whispered.

His eyes sparkled. 'Aye, I have this effect oan th' lassies.'

She slapped his shoulder, and he bent down to kiss her again.

The patio door slid open.

'Oh, here you are. Angus, you promised me a dance before I leave and I'm afraid these old hips won't last much longer.' Rose's Great Aunt Gertrude tapped him on the shoulder. 'Do you mind, young Rose, if I steal your cousin away?' she asked.

'Cousin?' They both chorused.

'What did I say? Come on.' Aunt Gertrude took Angus's arm, forcing him through the patio doors back into the reception.

Rose stood against the wall, breathing harder, tears threatening to come. She gripped the wall behind her. Equal parts elated and disgusted by the feelings running through her body. She put her head in her hands.

'Oh no,' she moaned.

Lily stumbled out on to the patio squealing, her dancing partner followed her out, playing her bottom like a drum and making neighing horse noises. Seeing Rose slumped against the wall Lily slapped his hands away.

'Rosie, what's the matter?'

The man slunk away. 'I'll leave you girls be.'

'He's our cousin.' Rose sobbed into her cupped hands.

'Who?' asked Lily, taking Rose by the shoulders.

'Angus.'

'No, that can't be right. Oh, hang on, I guess he is Uncle Jock's son.'

'Aunt Gertrude just told me.'

'Oh well, you don't have to like him just because he's family.'

Rose looked up and wailed.

'What? Has something happened?' Lily's eyes widened. 'You haven't done anything with him, have you?'

Rose cupped and covered her face once more. 'No, I mean yes, I mean no.'

Lily tilted Rose's chin up to meet her eyes. 'Look at me. What happened?'

'We kissed.'

'Minging,' Lily screwed up her pretty face.

'I know,' Rose said, burying her cheeks back into her hands.

An announcement through the megaphone by the DJ caught their attention. 'Ladies, back to the dance floor please, time to throw the bouquet.'

Lily took her hand. 'Come on.'

Rose shook her head.

'You have to.'

Her body turned to Angus like a homing pigeon as soon as she re-entered the room. He leant against the wall, talking to one of her uncles. 'Their' uncles, she reminded herself. Her eyes met his, and she saw a mixture of pain and bewilderment reflected back. Lily dragged her to stand behind the first row of women who eagerly jostled forward for prime positions to catch Melanie's bouquet. Rose's hands hung limply by her side. Melanie tossed the bouquet and Lily yanked Rose's hand upwards, catching the flowers together. A group of men jostled forward as Melanie seated herself on a chair ready to throw her garter. Rose handed the bouquet to Lily and excused herself. She heard roars of male appreciation for Melanie's performance as she headed to the bathroom.

Rose stared in the mirror as she let the cool water run over her wrists. She yearned for her mother. Rose slipped her mobile phone out of her small silk bag and looked at the time. It would be early morning in England. She dialled.

'Mum.'

'Rosie, is that you love? How lovely. Has the wedding finished already?'

'No, Melanie is throwing her garter. I'm just having a bathroom break.'

'Did you catch the bouquet?'

'Yes, mum.'

'I knew it. Good girl, you'll be next. We could do with a good wedding.' She let her mother ramble on; it comforted her to hear her voice. 'Are you all right Rosie?'

'Yes, mum.'

'Well, you don't sound yourself, love.' Her mother's voice rose an octave. 'Is that Angus being awful to you again?'

'No mum, actually he's been, well, quite nice actually.' Rose closed her eyes.

'You sound surprised. I expect he's grown up quite a lot. So like your Uncle Jock, that one.'

Rose leant against the tiles. 'So, it's true he is my cousin, then?'

'I guess you could say that.'

'Why didn't you tell me?' she hissed, trying to control her tone.

'I didn't think about it.'

Rose didn't want to start an argument. 'It's okay, mum.'

'It's not like we see them anymore.'

'I know.' Rose heard the music start up. 'Look, I'd better go, mum.'

'I wish I could have been there; did you explain to Melanie?'

Rose rolled her eyes. 'Yes mum, she understands you can't leave Nan.'

'Did Uncle Jock make it?'

'No, bad heart, apparently. Angus came on his own.'

'That man never did himself any favours with his drinking. I had quite the thing for him back in the day.'

'Mum.'

137

'Oh, don't be silly, love. It was before your father swept me off my feet. We were all good friends.'

'That's minging. He's still my uncle. Bye mum. Got to go. Love you.' She raised her finger to end the call.

'Not by blood, he's not.'

'What? What did you say?' Rose pressed the phone to her ear.

'Like I said, we were all close. We called him your Uncle Jock since the day you were born. He's your Godfather, not really your uncle.'

'You never told me that.'

'He wasn't much of a Godfather. Your father didn't approve of my choice, so we never really talked about it after your christening.'

'So, he's not my cousin?

'No love.'

'Thanks mum, love you. I've got to go.' Rose rammed the phone back into her silk pouch and ran out of the bathroom.

She found Angus on the dance floor doing an awkward, slow dance with Aunt Gertrude. Rose pushed her way through the grinding bodies and tapped Aunt Gertrude on the shoulder.

'My turn to cut in.'

'Thank goodness, I think my knees are going to cave.' She pecked Rose's cheek and shuffled away.

Rose grabbed the lapels of Angus's suit jacket, pulling him towards her, kissing him full on the mouth. She pulled away enjoying the surprised look on his face. 'We are not related, not by blood, I mean,' she shouted over the music.

His eyes widened. 'Are ye sure?'

She nodded. 'Mum just confirmed it.'

He grinned. Relief flooded her body. Angus grabbed her around the waist, lifted her up above his head and twirled her around, his kilt and sporran flying as he spun faster and faster.

She threw her head back and laughed. When she looked down into his eyes, he lowered her feet to the floor, swung her up into his arms, and cradled her body to his. The sandals slipped from her feet, clattering to the dance floor.

Angus Rory carried Rose in his arms towards the exit and ran down the stone steps leading to the garden. He lowered her onto the manicured lawn. The cool, wet grass underfoot sent a shiver through her slight frame. He removed his kilt jacket and placed it around her shoulders.

Rose ran her hands down his biceps and up again, encircling his neck. He bent forward and crushed his lips to hers. His hands moved down Rose's sides and over her bottom.

Her fingers ran down his torso, to the hem of his kilt. She pulled her hand away, looking into his deep blue eyes. He nodded and her hands travelled under his kilt.

A smile danced over her mouth.

KICKSTART MY HEART

debbie kahl

I 've always been the good girl. But when I take the chance to blow that off, I make very bad choices. Which is kind of how I ended up here, naked and sated in the bed of the boy whose heart I broke at sixteen. Granted, he's definitely not a boy anymore, given we're both in our mid-forties and there were no nervous, first time fumblings this time around, but we're both also going through ugly divorces. From other people. We certainly don't need any complications in what's already a very complicated and drama riddled situation. Which makes this a really, really bad decision. We should be home alone, in separate beds, licking our wounds, not each other. I'm not even sure how it happened. Well, actually, that's a lie. I know exactly how it happened.

It all started when I scurried home to my parents, to hide out in my childhood bedroom and curse at the universe, because my ex-husband's mistress had just given birth to their baby girl. After a decade of trying to have a baby of our own and failing miserably, despite spending a fortune on medical appointments, IVF, hormones and fertility tests which never achieved anything, he managed to knock her up pretty quickly. Right about the time my doctor confirmed I was in perimenopause and, despite the desperate whirlwind of medical treatments I'd tried over the last decade to be a mum, the reality was I'd probably never have children of my own. Thank you very much endometriosis, you evil witch. And, when you added this to the announcement that he didn't love me anymore and was leaving to have a baby, with *her*, it almost pushed me over the edge. Actually, it did push me over the edge. So, I did the only responsible thing a woman in her mid-forties would do when her world fell apart. I drank myself into oblivion night after night, and when that didn't work, I ran home to Mum and Dad. And straight into the paint-stained arms of my high school boyfriend. Well, not literally at first but you know, things happen when you're lonely and desperate.

I guess that was the problem with growing up in a small town, where everyone lived in each other's business. Of course, my parents would employ the man whose heart I shattered as a teenager to paint their house. They love him, they've always loved him, and they've never forgiven me for dumping him and choosing life in the big city instead of a hometown life with the town painter and a tribe of tiny terrors. Well, the joke was on me, wasn't it? After arriving under the cover of darkness on the final flight out, I slunk back into town, snuck into my parent's house, crawled into my childhood bed, and slept the best I have in months.

Or I was, until Mötley Crüe's 'Kickstart My Heart' blasting at full volume shook my bedroom walls and dragged me, quite rudely, from my slumber. What the feck? This couldn't be happening. I came home for peace and quiet and I was met with eighties hair metal music at seven in the morning?

When the groaning and hiding under my pillow didn't work, trust me I tried, I pulled the bedroom door open with more force than was probably necessary and smacked into the bare chest that filled my doorframe. A very muscular, bare chest tinged with the lightest shimmer of sweat that hinted at the summer heatwave we were in. I looked up and stared into the pale blue eyes of Mark Henderson. Eyes that still bore into my soul. And when his cheeky smirk that's always managed to melt me lit up his face in recognition, it kickstarted my heart indeed.

'Morning Abby,' he said, barely containing a chuckle. 'This is unexpected. You're looking … well.'

I couldn't miss the pause. Why did he pause? I pushed past him and faced myself in the bathroom mirror opposite my bedroom. What stared back at me could be best described as zombie apocalypse Abby. Urgh, I really should have taken my makeup off before I went to bed last night, raccoon eyes and smudged lipstick is never a good look.

I felt Mark behind me before I met his eyes in the mirror.

'Rough night?' he asked.

'Rough year.'

'Yeah, I hear you on that.' He paused, as his ice blue eyes reacquainted themselves with my body. My much curvier, carrying more weight than I'd like, perimenopausal body. It's definitely different to how it was when I was sixteen, given my curves and boobs didn't bother showing up until my twenties.

I was suddenly very aware that sleeping in my underwear was probably not the best choice, but it was too late now. And given how prone I am to impromptu hot flashes, especially in this sticky weather, he should have been grateful I didn't sleep naked. Wait … Let's not go there. Especially since Mark's eyes devoured me as he looked me up and down before moving a foot closer.

The air crackled, like we were in some cheesy romance novel, and Mark leant forward to whisper in my ear.

'So, Abby, what are you doing here? You know your parents are out of town while I'm painting the house, right?'

'What?' I grabbed the bench in front of me to keep myself upright. The heat from that whisper stood every hair on the back of my neck at attention.

'Your parents, you know they're not here, right?' Mark continued, his eyes still roaming as he moved even closer, if that's at all possible. So close he could've licked the side of my face if he wanted. Not that I was into that kind of thing but he could've.

'No. I didn't know. Where are they?' I squeaked. So much for oozing confidence and sophistication. One whisper and a good eye devouring and I was oozing something, but it wasn't confidence.

'They went to visit your aunt. Decided it would be better to get out of the house while I was painting, given the mess and the fumes. They didn't tell you?'

'No. They didn't. So much for surprising them,' I muttered under my breath.

'Well, you've surprised me, so I guess that's something.'

'Yeah, you've surprised me too.' I giggled, more out of nerves than anything else.

144

'So, I guess you'll just have to stay here and be my helper. Cater to my every whim.'

'Yeah.' I giggled again as Mark winked at me. 'But I'm not really sure you're talking about painting.'

'Abby, I'm definitely not talking about painting.'

My heart accelerated. It'd been so long since anyone has shown any romantic interest in me, I wasn't quite sure how to react—although fear and panic with a twinge of excitement seemed to be topping the list if the rapid heartbeat was any indication.

'Oh, um, I'm not really sure I'm up for that, yet,' I managed to stammer out.

'Pity. From what I remember, we were good together. *Really good.*'

'Yeah, we were really good,' I said because let's face it, I might be less than perfect but I wasn't going to lie.

'Still could be,' Mark said with a shrug. 'Not sure what's happened to the girl I knew, or where that spark has gone? But you know where to find me if you change your mind.'

And with that, he was gone. If it was at all possible, the music outside the door cranked up even louder.

I wasn't sure if it was meant to tease or torture me but Mötley Crüe's 'Home Sweet Home' blasting through the doorway reminded me I was neither on my way, nor set free. So much for the girl who was going to set the world on fire. No, she was too busy hiding in her parents' bathroom.

I glared at my freshly washed reflection in the mirror, twisting and turning to look at myself from all angles. No matter which way I looked at it, being the eternal good girl had gotten me nowhere. So many sacrifices, so many missed opportunities, so many times I had said yes when I really meant no, and so much self-loathing. And for what? To be the good girl, the good wife, furthering someone else's career at the expense of my own. Little Miss Reliable. I've always done everything for everyone else and where has that got me? Absolutely fricken nowhere. Well, feck that. I've had enough of being Little Miss Perfect. Just once I wondered what it'd be like to be Little Miss Naughty. To just do whatever and whoever I want, whenever I want and not overthink it.

I looked out the bathroom door and watched Mark, his back to me as he painted the wall opposite, humming along to the music. His seriously sexy muscles and his shoulders, broadened with age, played havoc with my saliva glands. Not to mention that butt in those paint splattered jeans. He'd got a bit curvier in all the right places too. I licked the sweat away from my lips, or maybe it was drool. Who could tell in that heat, and who really cared anyway? He was hot and I was hot … for him.

As if he could feel me ogling every inch of him, he turned, folded his arms across that wicked chest I really did want to lick after all, and winked. And that smirk, I just wanted to kiss it right off his face, and then maybe move onto other things.

Oh my God, what was wrong with me? This was not me. This was bad girl Abby. And who knew where she'd been all those years, and why she decided to show up and give my slumbering libido a shake up, but bad girl Abby wanted to do very, very naughty things to the super-hot tradie in front of her.

'C'mon Abby,' Mark said, 'we're both single, we're both adults *and* we've done this before. Aren't you the least bit curious to know what it'd be like after all these years?' He finished this with a raised eyebrow.

Who knew a raised eyebrow could be so sexy but repressed bad girl Abby was a goner for that freaking raised eyebrow.

'Yes,' I managed to squeak out before Mark closed the gap between us in two steps and pulled me into his arms. His lips met mine and it really was like coming home. He still kissed like he did all those years ago, soft lips, just the right pressure and when he wrapped me in his arms, for the first time in years I felt safe and protected. Until I pushed him backwards into my bedroom and climbed him like a scratching pole. Bad Abby had been such a good girl, so patient and tolerant with my stupid decisions for all those years. I deserved to be rewarded and that reward, was Mark.

LOST. AND FOUND

angela victor

'It fits, but there's no way I'm wearing it,' I called out to Lauren. The tiny cubicle was cluttered with discarded Lycra and sequinned bits of jersey. I was running out of time to find a costume for the party.

'Lemme see,' she hollered back.

I sucked in my stomach, whipped back the faded dressing room curtain and struck a power pose.

Lauren looked up from her phone. 'Whoa!' Her eyebrows had shot to the ceiling.

I peered over my shoulder to check out the back view and gasped. Either the mirror was warped, or my grandmother's greatest fear had come to pass. *I'd let myself go.*

My pulse hammered double time, and the corner of my right eye started twitching.

'I'm gonna cancel,' I muttered. I hadn't wanted to go to Harry's party in the first place, but I'd promised my friend Amy I'd stop being such a hermit.

Lauren hauled herself from the purple velour beanbag for a closer inspection.

'You look amazing, Izzy,' she said to my cleavage. She looked up and gazed solemnly into my eyes. 'I would *so* do you.'

I snickered. 'Your standards are low these days.' Since breaking up with her ex, Lauren was rebounding around Brisbane like a basketball. She didn't discriminate. The only requirement was a skirt.

'Yes, but I'm getting laid. Maybe try it sometime?' She had a point. It had been a while. Okay, maybe quite a while, but I'd never been good at casual flings. I'm more of a serial monogamist.

Lauren adjusted the red vinyl belt, then gripped the top of my Wonder Woman costume and tugged it up. She stood back to admire her handiwork.

'I wouldn't make any sudden moves, if you know what I mean. Better tape the girls in.'

The costume shop guy wandered over. 'Whoa!'

Lauren grinned. 'That's what I said!'

'My butt looks like a watermelon,' I muttered—more like two.

I sucked in another deep breath, and my breasts almost overflowed out the top. Lauren was right. I needed tape— the heavy-duty, Gaffer kind. Was there enough time to get to Bunnings?

'That's why superheroes wear capes—it's all about coverage,' costume guy tutted, attaching a swathe of red velvet around my shoulders.

The cape boosted my confidence. I twirled and struck a superhero pose. Maybe I *could* pull this off, and I *did* have the perfect pair of boots at home.

'I'd kill to have an arse like yours,' Lauren said, flinging a feather boa around her neck. 'It's voluptuous. Lush. Kardashianesque. Unlike mine, flat as a pancake.'

'Yeah, mine too,' costume guy said. He and Lauren stood together, checking out their side profiles in the mirror. 'I need more lift,' he complained. 'Some days, my pants don't want to stay up. I was thinking about a BBL.'

'What's a BBL?' I asked.

'Brazilian Butt Lift,' they chorused.

'Or you could start wearing braces,' Lauren suggested. 'They're cheaper and y'know ... no downtime.'

'At least you fit into your pants,' I said, lifting the cape to check myself out again.

Lauren rolled her eyes. 'So, you put on a few kilos working from home. Who cares? You've put it on in all the right places. Your stomach's still pretty flat, and your arms look good.'

'Do you see this?' I grasped a chunk of leg. 'It's *cell-u-lite*. Dimpled skin only works for citrus, Lauren.'

'And babies,' costume guy chimed in. I gave him a narrow-eyed look.

'Meh. So, wear some tights,' Lauren said. 'You look fab!' She tried on a giant sombrero and admired herself in the mirror.

'Get a spray tan,' costume guy suggested. 'Tanned fat instantly transforms into muscle, you know.' He spoke with tremendous authority.

Maybe he was right. I *was* looking pasty, practically ill. Some colour wouldn't go astray, and nor would some instant muscle. I'd been meaning to get to the gym, but I'd been busy. Busy at work, busy building up my side hustle, busy watching Netflix, and very busy watching cat videos on Insta.

'If you want to drench your body in toxic chemicals to give the illusion of sun damage, go right ahead, but I have to get going. I've got a date,' Lauren said.

She grasped my shoulders and gave me a series of confidence-rousing shakes. 'The outfit's amazing ... you're guaranteed to pull ... my work here is done.'

I walked into Harry's penthouse a few hours later, solo. Amy had cancelled last minute because of a work drama, but I'd decided to go anyway. Enough hermitting.

The party was in full swing. Dozens of silver balloons bobbed along the high ceiling, and Gaga blared from the speaker. Superheroes mingled on the terrace, sprawled on leather lounges, and a few danced on the parquetry floor. Captain America shimmied against Super Girl, Robin draped himself over Iron Man, and Thor gyrated against his hammer.

I wished I'd come as the Invisible Woman and decided to make a run for it before anyone saw me.

'Whoa! Nice costume, Izzy.'

Too late. I turned and smiled my dazzling smile, the wide one with loads of teeth.

Harry gave me an appreciative once-over, and I gave him one back. Surely not all those muscles were padded. And as for his jaw, he must be chewing a lot of gum these days. Very chiselled.

'Amy coming?' he asked.

'Work emergency.'

'That's too bad.' The intensity of his stare unnerved me, so I shoved the gift bag towards him.

'Welcome to the dirty thirties, Harry. Happy birthday!' It was some aftershave and a pair of *'Let's par-tee'* socks. I heard he still played golf.

'Aw, thanks. You shouldn't have.' He leant down to kiss me, and his chin whacked into my nose, making my eyes water. He threw back his head and laughed off the awkward moment with that confident way he had about him.

'Let me get you a drink, babe.' His white teeth gleamed against his naturally swarthy tan. I asked for champagne, but what I really wanted was an ice pack for my nose.

'Champas it is!' He waggled a finger. 'I don't care if some orphan child is in peril or an entire city needs saving from a flesh-eating plague, you're not to move from this exact spot, yeah? I'll be right back.'

His attention was overwhelming, but when had I last been to a party? And apart from the guy who usually delivered my Amazon packages, it had been a while since anyone had flirted with me like that. I needed to get out more.

While I waited for Harry to return, I made small talk with a few people I hadn't seen since high school — Cat Woman, two Hulks and a heavily pregnant Supergirl — and soon started questioning my life. They had partners. I was single. They were adopting kids, starting families. I was building a career. Kind of.

Besides, there was no rush. I was only thirty. There was still time — *so much time.* I decided to research freezing my eggs.

It's not that I was against settling down with someone, but the lucky someone hadn't shown up. I thought they had, but that was years ago, and we were both too young. *Brendan-The-American-Exchange-Student.* He'd exchanged my heart for a lump of coal and left, never to be seen again. I hadn't experienced that same level of connection with anyone since.

Harry reappeared, clutching two glasses and a bottle of Veuve.

'Let's sit on the terrace and have a private birthday toast to me.' He gave me a wink. 'We can start toasting you when we get to the second bottle.'

A private toast? I'd only known Harry to date edgy, sophisticated types and emaciated models. Surely I was misreading the signals?

Harry regaled me with entertaining stories about his clients while I guzzled champagne. He'd become a barrister a few years ago and had no qualms defending the bad guys.

He told me about a burglar wanting to sue an old lady after he fell through her skylight. He'd crash-landed on her fish tank and cut himself to pieces. I laughed so hard my head started hurting, then it became fuzzy. Very fuzzy.

I peered at my glass.

154

'Did you put something in this?' I asked in a joking kind of way, not wanting to offend him. Harry had been a renowned party boy back in the day, but spiking drinks?

'Just a little something to take the edge off, Iz. Enjoy.' He smirked, and I froze.

What? A curl of fear twisted in the pit of my stomach, and that scene in *Pulp Fiction*, the one where Uma Thurman's character lies unconscious on the floor, flashed through my head. My heart skipped a beat and I broke into a light sweat.

'Relax,' he said and looked down at his phone.

I stumbled to my feet.

'You ...' I pointed my finger at Harry, which was tricky because now there were two of him. '... are an *arsehole!*'

The word reverberated, echoing in my head.

He gestured at me with his champagne glass. 'Right there. That's what I'm talking about. You need to learn to chill, babe.'

A pouty-lipped Captain Marvel slunk over and whispered something in his ear. They laughed, and Harry gave me a wry look before pulling the girl into his lap.

She gave my outfit a once over with a sulky glance. 'Cool boots,' she murmured and popped a Chupa Chup in her mouth.

Harry grinned up at me. 'Don't go, Dizzy Izzy,' he said. 'Stay. We can all have fun in the Bat Cave, yeah?'

'Grow up, Harry.' What an arsehole.

'Izzy, I'm sorry!' he called out, but I continued back inside. I needed to go home.

The party had become boisterous, and the heat was oppressive. One of the Green Lanterns bounded over. 'Wonder Woman! Darling! We're in desperate need of a red cape. Do you mind?'

'Take it,' I said and without the burden of the fabric, was so much cooler. Who needed coverage?

Green Lantern screamed, 'El Toro! El Toro!' and held my cape out to one side like a Spanish Matador. A few guys began snorting like bulls and taking turns galloping through it, roaring with laughter.

The 'Nutbush' song started, and the room burst into a cheer. More people surged forward to dance, hemming me in. I had to get out. It felt like popping candy was exploding in every cell of my body.

Someone called my name, and as I spun toward the voice, the tape holding my costume up gave way. A scream froze in my throat, and somebody grabbed me before I could even cover myself.

'I've got you,' the guy said, holding my head against his chest, shielding my nakedness.

I kept my eyes squeezed shut, wishing the night away. *Could it get any worse?*

'No one saw you. They're all bombed.' The movement of his lips tickled my ear, and even from the depths of my mortification, I noticed the American accent.

Whoever he was, he smelt delicious. The scent was something good, something familiar. I couldn't quite place it.

I slipped my arms around his waist and clung on like a limpet. His body was big and comforting, his heartbeat steady against my thrashing one.

'Shhh, it's okay,' he soothed. 'Look at me?'

I made a noise like a wounded animal and shook my head. My wardrobe failure was bound to wind up on social media any minute. I'd decided to stay glued to him forever.

'I'll ease off my coat and wrap it around you, okay?' He spoke with calm authority, the way you'd talk to someone strapped to a bomb with only ten seconds on the clock.

Who was this guy? Curiosity got the better of me, and I opened my eyes to take a quick peek. *Oh, a Clarke Kent.*

Wait a minute! My head snapped back up.

'Brendan?' His name came out in a strangled squeak. It couldn't be! He was gone. Long gone. And this Brendan was different. Older, bigger.

He shrugged off his Clarke Kent trench coat and wrapped it around my shoulders, holding it bunched at my throat while I manoeuvred into the sleeves.

'Yes, Iz. It's me.'

I stared at him in wonder. He'd always been handsome, but now? He was beautiful. Memories of our year together skittered through my mind—the laughter, the chess games, the falling in love, the heartbreaking goodbye at the airport.

Everyone promised the pain of losing him would pass, but they'd lied. My heartache had expanded into a chasm of forever, dulling but never dissolving.

I didn't know if it was the drug or the shock of seeing him, but nausea set in. I was either going to vomit or pass out.

'I've got to get out of here,' I mumbled. I'd already lost my top, and there was no way I was losing the contents of my stomach in front of this crowd as well.

I began weaving towards the elevator. The last thing I remember before blacking out was Brendan scooping me into his arms and asking, 'Where's home these days?'

A cackle of laughter nudged the edge of my consciousness, but I pushed the shrill sound from my mind, holding on to the dream. I was swimming back to shore, cool salty water lapping over my body, the hot summer sun on my back. The guy on the beach smiled and waved, but I couldn't see who was behind the sunglasses.

More cackles. *Kookaburras?* Weird. I'd never heard kookaburras at my place before. The dream slipped away, and I stretched, wiggling my toes into the warm, soft sheets, wishing it was sand.

The toaster popped, and my coffee machine gurgled. I stiffened. The coffee machine was *broken*. My eyes flew open, took in the unfamiliar bedroom and snapped shut again. I held my breath and kept still, sensing someone looming over me.

'Stop foxing. I can tell you're awake, Izzy. Coffee?'

I exhaled, not knowing where I was but knowing with absolute certainty that I was safe. It hadn't been a dream. Brendan had come back!

I pulled the doona tight beneath my chin and gazed up at him.

He wore boxers, his long lanky legs now muscled and well-defined, and a crumpled white linen shirt stretched over broad shoulders. The top few buttons were undone, revealing dark curling hairs, and I had an irresistible urge to touch them.

He perched on the edge of the bed and looked at me. Even his eyes had changed, their earnest intelligence shining with more intensity and confidence than I remembered.

His lazy smile zinged low in my belly. The handsome young guy I'd once lost was now very much a man. A sexy man.

'How are you feeling, Iz?'

Um, unravelled. 'Splitting headache,' I muttered, and he winced in sympathy.

'I've got Tylenol.'

'What are you doing here, Brendan? Why are you back?'

'Work. I flew in yesterday.'

'Oh.' I'd heard he'd become a hotshot New York executive.

'I found out from Chris you'd be at the party last night, and I had to find you.'

I didn't know they'd kept in touch. Hang on a minute. *Find me?* I'd been here the whole time, right where he'd left me. The old pain tasted bitter in my mouth, but I'd always known the deal. Australia for one year and then on to Africa to volunteer for another year, which had stretched into two, and by that time, we were dating other people.

'Listen, as much as I'd love to catch up on old times, I'd better get moving.' I wasn't in the market for more heartache. I was already stocked up. I peered under the doona and groaned when I saw the Wonder Woman remains.

159

'I'll get you something to wear,' Brendan said, pulling some clothes from an expensive-looking duffel bag. 'Iz, do you really have to go?' His eyes were pools of dark, liquid heat.

'I ...' My throat went dry.

'Why not stay for a while? We could hang out.'

The fluttering in my stomach intensified into an all-out flap, threatening to levitate me off the bed. How could I say no?

'Maybe. Just for a bit,' I said, biting my bottom lip.

He nodded, satisfied. 'I'll leave you to get dressed, or ...' he gave me a grin, 'by all means, keep wearing the suit.'

'You're kidding, right?' He held my gaze and slowly shook his head.

'You? In that outfit last night? Damn, Izzy.' He gave a low whistle and left the bedroom, taking my wits with him. I had to get a grip.

The marble bathroom was luxurious and well-appointed. I repaired my face and hair as best I could and changed into a pair of his cotton boxers and a faded NYU T-shirt.

I found him sprawled on the couch, scrolling through his phone.

He looked up and stilled, his eyes holding mine. I pretended to show interest in the apartment.

'Whose place is this? It's gorgeous.' It must be one of those converted lofts near New Farm, based on the view of the river outside.

I sat opposite him to put some space between us and to stop myself from crawling into his lap.

'Airbnb. If I stay in one more hotel, I'll go mad.' He gestured towards the chessboard on the low glass table between us. 'Wanna play?'

'We haven't seen each other in over a decade, and you want to play chess?'

He arched an eyebrow. 'Afraid of humiliation? Annihilation?'

'You might like to recall who won the last game,' I said with a laugh, and with that, the last of my resistance evaporated. I started setting up the ivory pieces while he finished making coffee. Maybe it was just me who remembered everything.

He took a phone call, and I overheard he'd be flying out Thursday. *So soon?* My chest squeezed, which was ridiculous. There'd never been any hope of a future with Brendan, not then and not now. End of story.

The rest of the day passed by as if we'd never been apart.

We listened to jazz, played chess and talked about his life in New York and mine in Brisbane. He gave me ideas for my online art business and showed me pics of his swanky new apartment. We argued over what ingredients belonged on a hamburger and who had the worst lockdown experience. We laughed so much my stomach muscles ached.

Later, we dropped by my place so I could change clothes. I agonised over what to wear and settled on an emerald green wrap-around dress. Sexy, but elegant.

Brendan was waiting for me on the balcony, taking in the lights of Brisbane's city skyline.

'Wow. You're stunning,' he said, his eyes darkening.

161

'Thanks.' I felt myself blush. 'You look pretty good yourself.' Ha! Understatement of the century. He might as well have stepped from a GQ photo shoot. Tall, dark and devastatingly handsome.

I'd snagged a dinner reservation at a cosy new Thai place in the Valley. We'd talked all day without taking a breath, but sitting across from him in the restaurant? I couldn't think of a single thing to say.

He picked at his food, I picked at mine. I had no idea what we ordered.

I kept looking at his hands, imagining them on me. So big, so capable. I suppressed a groan, took another gulp of wine, and tried not to squirm on the chair.

'Do you want to get out of here?' His voice had dropped a couple of octaves.

'Desperately,' I said.

It was a silent ride back to his place. He locked the front door, tossed down the key and turned towards me with hooded eyes.

'Isabella.' My name on his lips shot a thrill up my spine.

In two strides, he had me pressed against the wall. Cradling my head with one hand, he gripped my waist with the other, and slanted his mouth across mine.

The kiss undid me.

My handbag dropped with a thud to the floor, and my knees buckled. He held me tighter and hitching my leg around his hip, deepened the kiss. I moaned, melting into his hardness, my heart bursting from my chest. The taste of him was like coming home.

We didn't leave the apartment for the next three days.

Being with him was like finding the last piece of your jigsaw puzzle beneath the table—that perfect feeling of rightness when the lost piece slots into the picture.

Brendan was my missing piece.

And then he was gone.

Again.

I huddled in the plastic seat at the Qantas departure gate, drowning in bone-crushing grief. How was it possible to feel this much pain when I'd known all along he was going? The ache in my chest expanded, and the tears finally fell.

I tried to ignore the sounds of a commotion behind me.

'Izzy!'

Brendan? I swung around to see him running towards me. *What on earth was he doing?*

'Excuse me, sir. You already boarded! Please return to the plane immediately.' The harried flight attendant was right behind Brendan, and a security guard barked into her walkie-talkie.

'Brendan, what is it? Are you okay? Did you forget something?'

'No! I'm not okay,' he growled, hauling me up from the chair and holding my face between his hands. 'And I forgot nothing. That's the problem, Izzy. I tried, but I could never forget you and I just don't have it in me to leave you again.' His eyes reflected my own misery.

163

'Brendan, you live *there*, and I'm *here*.' I knew I was ugly crying, but I couldn't stop.

'Geography can't rule our lives, Izzy.'

I pushed his hands away from my face in frustration. 'But the law *does!* I can't get a visa for the States, and you can't get one here,' I wailed. 'We went through all this years ago.'

'My wife could get a green card.'

His what? His *wife?* What the hell was he talking about? My heart dropped like a lead weight to my toes. I couldn't believe it. The bastard was *married!*

'Are you trying to tell me you're *married?*' I shoved him, and he stumbled backwards.

'No!' He laughed. 'But I think I should be. To you, Iz.'

'*What?*' My heart lurched.

'What we had was not some silly teenage love. It was real and true and deeper than the fucking Pacific Ocean that lies between us.' He thumped his fist against his chest. 'And it's all still here.'

He dropped down onto one knee and clasped my hand between his. My jaw dropped.

'Isabella Jane Thomas, say you'll be mine. Please do me the honour of becoming my wife.'

'Sir, I need you to return to the plane.' The attendant sounded less certain.

'*Izzy?*' His eyes frantically searched mine.

I nodded, and then I was back in his arms. It was all very Hollywood, except for my streaky mascara and dripping nose.

'Way to go, mate!' someone yelled, and the small crowd of onlookers cheered when he kissed me.

With that, a bunch of burly security guards turned up in a golf buggy.

One year later ...

We were awake but still in bed when the siren started blaring outside. It was true. New York never slept.

'Whatever happened to that Wonder Woman suit, hmm?' Brendan's lips nuzzled my neck and trailed down towards my breasts.

'As if I'd fit into it now,' I grumbled.

He gave me a sleepy smile and slipped his hand beneath the covers to rest against my impossibly large belly. The baby responded with a series of karate kicks and a few punches.

'I think our kid has the makings of an action hero,' he said.

'A super baby,' I sighed and started to doze off again.

THE DESERT FLAME

jared kranz

A foreign city, deep within the desert. Its isolation and outside trade were at first both exotic and opportunistic for Dari. Now, as he hugged sandstone walls to avoid the soon-to-be unbearable midday sun, pushing his way through crowded alleys and bazaars wreaking of pungent meats and body odours, he knew better. His original plan had him staying several more days but upon finally closing his trade with the Sultan, he saw no reason to extend his suffering. No reason but one and, if what his men had said was true, he needed to move quickly.

For the most, people parted way. His expensive silk shirt, gifted by local merchants, painted him as someone of importance but it was the way it fit loosely over his broad shoulders and heavy chest that indicated he was a man not to be trifled with. Deep blue eyes, framed in shadows by dark shoulder length hair, scanned his surroundings as he moved through the masses. Lost among the twists and turns that led everywhere and nowhere at once, he now followed the sound of callous jeers and taunts, familiar in any language. He forced his way down a tight alleyway, jumping several wicker baskets only to exit into yet another opening this one filled with market stalls, buyers and beggars. He ignored them, pushing his way through the crowd, cursing at what lay before him.

A circle of men, women and children looked on, with some taking part in the humiliation of a young woman huddled within its centre. Last night she had been disowned by the Sultan, a man who cared little for his people and treated his subjects as objects. Word had it that, upon returning to her former home, she had found herself unaccepted by those she grew up with. Having left the streets behind in search of a better life within the palace, the locals of her youth now resented and belittled her for it. Dari cared little for the history and customs of their people. He had come for her and, now that he had found her, his heart swelled at the sight and broke at her harrowing condition.

Reaching the circle, his mere presence silencing the jeers. Those closest to the girl stepped back, anticipating a reaction. The girl didn't notice. She remained hunched, one arm protecting her head, the other across her side, a simple ripped and torn dress all that protected her from the harsh rays of the sun. Dari looked at the bruises on her arms and legs and a pang of guilt overwhelmed him. His role in her fall from grace had been unintentional, but that didn't prevent him from believing it to be his fault.

There were no laws against a dancer sleeping with a foreigner, and in truth, had she come to him as a concubine there would have been no issues. But Dari had not slept with the woman named Arena. They had not even spoken. Yet all present in the tent had witnessed and felt the fire of their attraction as she danced, at first for a crowd of men, then for only one.

Dari and a dozen other guests had been invited to dine with the Sultan beneath a large canvas tent set beyond the walls of the city. Each on their own thatch mat, they had sat cross-legged, the space in-between dimly lit by oil lamps. Thin strands of aromatic smoke rose from small incense cauldrons, hung on long chains from the ceiling, their odour at times overwhelming. A guest from a far-off land, he was showered with gifts of fine cloth and lightly spiced wines. As the entertainment started, he watched, amused but mostly disinterested by the exotic dancing of barely clad women.

Then Arena had arrived.

Dark hair, her body tanned and lithe, her movements athletic yet graceful. He had studied her as closely as he had ignored the others, mesmerised by the way she moved, her body caressing the cooling desert night. Somehow, she wrapped herself equally in those finger-like tendrils of smoke as she did her pink silk scarf, a ghostly image too perfect to be real.

Their eyes met, perhaps unconsciously at first but soon without doubt, as the dance gravitated towards him. He remained still, locked in her trance. It was then, that everyone realised the mysterious woman no longer danced for the Sultan's men, but for him alone, the smoke tendrils unravelling as she swayed in the confidence of her near nakedness. She danced for him for there were no others. Two lonely souls trapped in a desert oasis, the harsh sands of time bringing them together against all odds. The silk pink scarf, all that remained of her modesty, was gracefully unravelled from her body. Her last armour against the night flung towards him alone, landing in his lap and letting him know that she was his. And without a doubt, he had known that he, too, was hers.

A bell tolled. Arena, locked in her own trance, had refused to stop dancing, the other girls forced to grab her and turn her away. When she vanished, the spell was broken. The harsh desert night imploded upon Dari as the entertainment ceased. The connection with the foreigner was obvious but the word was Arena was one of the Sultan's favourites. Dari questioned his hosts about the woman, but the men refused to provide answers, citing customs and beliefs, cautioning him for his own safety.

Now, finding the woman battered and broken, Dari broke through the circle that surrounded her. The crowd parted for this strange man in his even stranger garbs, the heavy crunch of his riding boots provided a slow steady rhythm towards her. His heart hammered in his chest, the sun suddenly hot on his face, the taste of sweat on his lips.

At the sound of footsteps Arena buried her head further into her arms, flinching at the shadow towering over her, unsure whether to protect her face or body from further blows. From his chest pocket, Dari removed the silk scarf that lain hidden within and tossed it before the cowering woman. It unravelled in its flight, dancing and fluttering through the air, graceful as its original owner, before landing lightly in front of her. The arm covering her head, slow and steady, reached out. As her fingers took comfort in the soft material, she turned her head to seek its origin.

The man stood there in the light, golden from the morning's sun, glorious and defiant to her own people's customs. His figure broad and strong, it reminded her of the paintings in the palace, of the heroes and legends who defied man and God alike. His strength was there for all to see, but it was his eyes that she remembered. The deepest blue, like an ocean she had only ever heard of in stories, eyes that told of a lifetime of learning and wisdom, but also of sincerity and truth, of heartbreak and new love. Of a soul, bruised and battered as her own. Two puzzle pieces that, when placed together, painted a picture so beautiful no one would dare separate them again. No words passed his lips, but a smile formed as he reached down. She moved to meet him, letting her hand fall in his.

Gently he helped her rise, supporting her weight. As she went to take her first step, she winced, stumbling from the wounds and bruises to her side. Dari caught her, sliding his arm firmly around her waist and pulling her towards him. She did the same, pressing their bodies together.

The crowd watched in stunned silence. Somehow not understanding but knowing all the same that something more important than their own prejudices was taking place. The couple didn't notice. Like last night, the world melted away and everything in time and space ceased to exist but them.

Arena's head was buried in his chest. After lost moments of listening to his heartbeat, the rise and fall of his powerful chest, she finally looked up, finding solace in his eyes. At last, she spoke.

'Why?'

'Because you are worth it.'

She closed her eyes at the response and somehow nestled deeper into him.

'I knew you would come.'

Her accent sent shivers down his spine.

'How could I not?'

171

Somewhere in the distance a trumpet blasted, whether for them, they did not know. The locals did, however. They stirred and shifted nervously away.

Concern rose in her eyes. 'I am banished from the palace, but they will not let me leave the city. The Sultan, he will kill us before allowing himself to lose face.'

'Then we will die together.'

'Is your life worth so little to you?'

'In truth, until last night, I had not realised I was truly alive.' One hand remained wrapped around her while the other caressed her cheek lightly. 'I am not so attached to the troublesome burden of life and its existence. Especially in your absence.'

He felt her soften against him, comforted by the warmth of his words. But there was an urgency in her reply.

'If we are to live, we must leave now.'

'My men are waiting at the eastern gate with horses.' He gave her a quick smile before pushing the loose lock of her hair back across her face and behind her ear. 'I had a feeling we might need to make a quick escape. Can you walk?'

'I will run like the wind if it means escaping these walls.'

Dari's hand slipped from her waist, tracing a line from the small of her back and down her forearm until he once again held her hand in his. With his body, he turned to face her side and, with a sweeping gesture of his free arm, pointed towards the east.

'Then, shall we?'

She grinned, her face coming alive, her eyes sparkling. 'We shall.'

They fled, a strange rush of fear for their safety mixed with a child-like edge of defiance. The trumpet blasts drew closer, but only reinforced their will to escape. Nothing would stop them living their new lives together, and before long, the east gate loomed above them. Dari led Arena to his men. With little time for introductions, he was handed the reins to his grey gelding, motioning for her to mount.

'I have never—'

'I will never let you fall.'

She nodded once and put her hands on his shoulder, his strong arms lifting her onto the saddle. He followed thereafter, shifting his weight behind her and manoeuvring their mount so they could look over the desert city one last time.

'Would you like to say goodbye to your old life?'

'What old life?' She looked across the dirty streets and the broken people, but the corner of her mouth lifted in a cheeky smile. 'Until moments ago, I had never truly lived.'

He laughed as he took the reins with one hand, the other firmly around her waist as he kicked the gelding's flank. The horse dipped its head, jolting forward into a fast trot before crossing the threshold of the gate into the great sands.

As the city disappeared behind the horizon, they slowed to a gentler pace, the rocking motion of the horse forcing their bodies into a deep, steady rhythm against each other. The dust did little to hide her sweet aroma, filling Dari's senses far stronger than that of the herbs the night before.

'Are you comfortable?'

'Yes.' It was barely a whisper.

They rode for maybe an hour as a group, before Dari and Arena veered from the party so the Sultan's guards would not find them amongst the caravan. If threatened, Dari's men could take care of themselves.

Later, when evening began to fall, the couple arrived at a small oasis. Dari secured the gelding, returning to find Arena standing under the faint glow of the setting sun. With one hand she played at the ragged dress, feeling what little protection it could offer. Surrounded by towering dunes, the world around them once again ceased to exist.

'The desert nights can be cold,' she warned.

Dari went to her, wrapping his arms around her shoulders, allowing her to feel the warmth of his body. She returned his embrace, their eyes meeting as his hand went to her cheek, tracing a line over her ear as he pushed the hair back from her face. His other arm slid down from the shoulders, feeling the curve of her back.

Arena's own fingers now traced the line of his shoulders, running slowly down his chest to the smooth muscles of his stomach.

'Somehow,' he replied, his lips moving dangerously close to hers, 'I don't think we are going to feel the cold.'

Though they had no fuel nor flint, their passion lit a fire the wind and chill of the desert night could not extinguish.

PLUS ONE

martin clancy

I tap my foot and glare daggers. 'You're late.'

'Fashionably late. Besides you said 8:30 it's only 8:32.' Although panting, he still manages to flash a cocky smile. He looks like he belongs on the billboard of an Abercrombie and Fitch advert. Though I suppose it also works for his line of work. He isn't necessarily stunning and isn't your stereotypical tan-and-abs kind of guy you see on television. Instead, he has a small stature and a bit of pudge. But his dimples, smile, confidence, and kind eyes make him very charming.

'Yes, but you should know that 8:30 means 7:30.'

'How would I know that?'

'Becky!' My aunt runs over, and I immediately stiffen as she scoops me up into a hug.

'Hello, Katharine.'

'You know it's Kathy for family and friends. Speaking of, who is this gorgeous man?'

She extends a hand for him to kiss and to my surprise, he doesn't miss a beat. 'Liam Shin, it's a pleasure to meet you, Becca has told me all about you.'

'Woohoo aren't you just a Prince Charming?'

'Should we go in now?' I chime in to break the trance he has on my aunt.

'Oh. Yes, yes let's go.' She leans into Liam's ear and whispers something, then saunters into the church. Looking over her shoulder and giving a wink before disappearing within.

I raise an eyebrow and look at Mr Prince Charming. 'What did she say?'

'Nothing, don't worry about it.' He chuckles to himself. 'She's … interested.'

'You mean interesting?'

'Yeah that, totally.' He laughs a bit more and I sigh and drag him into the church. He makes a joke about burning as my father comes over, eyes locked on Liam.

'The invitation said 8:30.' I try and look nonchalant, but his gaze burns into me.

'You know if you're not early you're late.' His voice is neutral, but I can feel his disappointment.

'This is Liam Shin, my boyfriend.'

He extends a hand to shake Liam's and to my horror Liam takes his hand and like my aunt kisses the back of it and gives the same charming allure … to MY FATHER!

'It's a pleasure to meet you sir.'

My dad glares. 'Are you mocking me boy?'

'No, no, he's not, he's just ... only just come to Brisbane yesterday.'

My dad raises an eyebrow. 'But you said you've been together for a year. And you have never left the country.'

I try to remain composed. 'I meant he's from Tasmania and he's not used to being in such a big city. That's a normal greeting for them, I met him on that business trip remember?'

He nods slowly and I hide my relief. 'We should find our seat.'

Liam sheepishly smiles and we hurriedly go to our seat with my father keeping eyes locked on Liam the whole way to the pews.

'Why did you do that?' I whisper through pursed lips.

'Sorry I wasn't thinking, Your dad is ... intense.'

'Is it just me or is he staring at me still?' I look over my shoulder, dad at the entrance to the chapel, still staring at Liam with narrowed eyes. I nod and slide closer to him making us seem as close as possible.

A hush comes over the room as 'I Will Always Love You' plays over a speaker.

My eyes keep on dad as he walks my sister, Stacy, down the aisle and throughout her partner's vows. He knows somehow, I just know it. Liam clasps my hand and I'm jolted out of my spiral. He is ...

'Are you crying?'

His words catch in his throat, 'They just are both so beautiful and happy and ...'

I roll my eyes but squeeze his hand.

The ceremony comes to an end as the two kiss and embrace.

We make our way to the after party. Liam doesn't let go of my hand the whole way. When I see my sister in the crowd, I drag him over to her.

'Stacy this must be ...' I gesture at her new wife.

'Izzy! Meet my sister Rebecca.'

Her now wife holds out a hand and firmly shakes mine, unlike my dainty blonde sister this woman is strong and covered in tattoos. She doesn't seem at all like my sister's type, more the type of person she'd date to antagonise our father.

'Pleasure.' I try to keep my tone civil, but by the narrowed-eyed look my sister gives me, tells me I failed.

'Becca, behave,' she warns.

Her wife gives a warm laugh. 'It's okay sweetheart, I'm sure she is just being protective of her little sister.'

At least she understands.

'You can't expect me not to be cautious. After all, I only found out you were getting married a few weeks ago, and I don't even know your new wife.'

'Can we not do this? Please,' she snaps, 'we're going to enjoy our wedding now if you'll excuse me.' She storms off and her wife gives us a wave before following her.

Liam tugs my arm. 'Hey, are okay?'

'I'm fine.'

'You're clearly not.'

I clench my fists. 'She just ... she never thinks things through.'

'I'm one hundred percent on her side for this one. You need to let her make her own decisions.'

'Aren't I paying you to be here?'

'Yeah, but do you want me to lie to you?'

I tense and shake my head. Without warning he gives me a firm embrace. 'It's okay,' he soothingly whispers into my ear.

'What ... What are you doing?' I can't help but blush.

He pulls back and looks me in the eyes, still holding my arms. 'She'll be okay, she seems really happy.'

I look up and my little sister does seem ... happy. Throughout our childhood, she was mostly angry or defiant. Mum passed when she was born and so it became my job to raise her. I was ten at the time. She had a temper and we clashed heads a lot. I don't think I have ever seen her smile like today. I thought, like everyone else, this whole thing was rushed, but now that I see how genuinely happy she is.

'I guess you have a point.'

He beams. 'See! Let's have fun, okay?'

I give in and my lip involuntarily curves. I can't help it, his smile is infectious ... like a rash.

The bride calls everyone over.

'Okay girls! Time for the flower toss!'

Liam pushes me over, but I shake my head and stand my ground.

'No. no, I'll pass.'

My sister looks disappointed.

'Come on, it's fun!' Liam encourages.

'You do it then.'

179

'Okay!'

'Wait, no ...'

'Come on we'll both do it.' He pulls me over and this time I let him.

Everyone crowds near the front, and I try hold back.

'Three ... Two ... One!'

The crowd cheers and girls pile on top of each-other and the bouquet falls directly into Liam's hands. I stare at him mouth agape. He beams and cheers. The girls join him and crowd around and I get pushed back. He laughs with everyone, and I move to a chair and slump. Tonight has been a shitshow. I rub my forehead. Why did I think hiring an escort to be my imaginary boyfriend would work? I should have just pretended to get sick or something. He emerges from the crowd and approaches the flower girl kneeling to her level. She beams when he says something, hands her the flowers and pats her head. She immediately runs off to show her mum. I smile, mum would have loved him. I wipe a tear away and straighten as he comes over.

'Can I have this dance?' He holds out his hand.

'We don't have to you know.'

'I'm asking because I want to.'

I look away and try to hide my blush. I take his hand and instead of me dragging him everywhere he leads me gently to the dance floor. The music immediately goes from upbeat uptown girl to 'I Will Always Love You'. I sigh at the cliché. Nevertheless, I do something that is very not me. I dance with a man I met only yesterday. And to be honest, I kind of love it. The summer heat makes me burn up. Or is that just him? Up close I really notice his deep brown eyes almost black. I feel my eyes getting lost in them. No, fuck. It's just the song and the closeness and him crying during the ceremony and being honest and funny and weird and no, no, no, this can't be happening, he's only here because I paid him. *Wake up Rebecca. I can't fall for him.*

'Why did you pick your line of work?' What's wrong with me? That's none of my business but I can't help but ask.

'To be honest, to save up for a house. I've been doing this forever, and because I am comfortable with people, it kind of worked out.'

'You do have a way with people. You're very sociable and empathic and your mood is ... contagious.' The last word comes out with more distain than I meant.'

'Thank you ... I think.' He chuckles.'

I feel almost thrown off. His goal is so ... responsible. I wasn't expecting anything like the response he gave. Hell, it would have made sense if he was going abroad or sky diving or some thrill-based activity, but he has the same goal as me.

'I'm saving for a place too, which means I work a lot, which makes meeting people difficult.' I admit 'I feel silly. It's not like me to do something like this. Tonight has actually been fun.'

'I'm glad. I really enjoy your company too.'

My face heats up and I look away.

'Hey ... Becca?'

'Yes.'

'There is something I wanted to—'

'Excuse me.' My dad puts a firm hand on Liam's shoulder and jolts me out of the trance.

181

'Dad, what's wrong?'

'I need to speak to Liam'.

Liam gives me a 'help me' expression but I just say, 'Okay, well don't be long dear.' I watch as my dad leads Liam off.

I turn over my shoulder. My sister is slow dancing with Isabella. I wish I could be as careless as she is. Just fall headfirst into love, but that's not how it works. Not for me.

'I said you need to leave.' Dad's voice travels over the music.

'Oh no. Fuck!' I run as fast as I can in the blasted high heels. 'Dad, what's wrong?'

'I'm sorry Rebecca, but he needs to leave.'

'What? Why?'

Liam is pale and obviously scared but holds his ground, 'Sorry sir, I can't leave, not without Becca.'

It's because he's paid to stay. Don't get your hopes up.

'You will leave and never talk to my daughter ever again!'

'Why?' I surprise myself with how loud I am.

'Your boyfriend is a prostitute. He lied, he doesn't live in Tasmania. He's from Brisbane.'

'What?' *How did he find out?*

'Liam ...' *I'm so sorry I ever put you through this and I like you I really do. You should leave. I have wasted your day.* That's what I want to say but I can't get it out.

'He doesn't love you, he is a liar and manipulator, and he needs to leave!' Dad is yelling, the music stops, and I feel everyone's eyes on me. I can't breathe.

My father turns to me, 'Tell him to go.' He is so angry. *Oh God, what have I done?*

182

I want to admit to the whole setup, but I can't. I can't face my father, instead all I manage to say is, 'Get out.'

'But ...' Liam looks shocked.

He's better off without me.

'Now. Get out!' I feel a rush of guilt and stop myself from crying. I know it's for the best. He should leave and never see me again. He's too good for me.

I feel my heart stab with pain as his puppy dog eyes burrow deep into my soul. He lowers his head and marches out. I feel my father's stare, deep and disappointed. I run to the bathroom and shut myself in a stall. And it all comes out. I sob.

'Becca?' My sister is soft and reassuring through the door. I open the stall and she kneels in front of me.

'Stacy, your dress.'

'Silly, you're more important than a dress.'

I try to stifle the sobs. 'I did something stupid, Stacy.'

'What?'

She looks so much like mum, they never met but are so alike.

'Liam ... I hired him to be my date, I only met him yesterday.' I sigh in relief and just pour out everything. About my ex-boyfriend, how awful he was, how we've been apart for a month, how my only friend suggested hiring someone to have fun, and how I hired him for the wedding to pretend to have my life together.

'I didn't want dad to know I'm a loser.' I sniffle.

She pulls me down to the floor to hug me. 'Sweetie, you're not alone.'

'I started to actually like him Stace. How sad is that? I'm such a wreck.'

'I don't think you're that bad. You're human. I say, go for it. He clearly likes you too. Apologise to him.'

'What's there to like? I'm bossy and shitty.'

'But you're honest and sincere, I think he saw that.'

'I'm so sorry Stacy.'

'For what?'

'Growing up, I was so controlling over you.'

'It's okay. I wasn't the best either. Remember that time I stuck gum in your hair, and you had to cut it into a bob? It looked awful, but you told dad you did it because you felt like a change. You always looked out for me. I love you and I know you love me too.'

I sweep Stacy into a hug and help her to her feet. She pats her dress, blows me a kiss, and leaves.

After a bit of breathing, I wash my face and runny makeup off. As I exit the bathroom back into the hall, I am greeted by people stealing secret glances and murmuring amongst themselves. I go to leave but my father cuts me off. Before he can say anything, I do what I should have done earlier. 'I hired him. I knew he was an escort and I brought him here to pretend to be my boyfriend. I lied.'

He stares at me with his jaw dropped. 'But ... why would you?'

'I knew I was always a disappointment. I could never be enough for you. I worked so hard to be what you wanted me to be. But I need to be me. I can't keep doing this, I can't keep living in your shadow.'

'I only want what is best for you.'

'What's best for me right now is to go home and work out how to make it up to Liam because he is what's best for me. He is kind and charming and funny and even if he doesn't like me back, I have to try.'

'The prostitute?' I can't tell if he's shocked or angry.

'Yes. Now excuse me.' I walk past him and make my way to my car.

Returning home, I think long and hard about how to make it up to him. I talk to Stacy and she helps me formulate a plan using her bountiful knowledge of rom-coms and soap operas. And that's why I'm standing at the front of Liam's house in the pouring rain. I throw a few pebbles at his window until he emerges and sees me.

'What are you doing out here?'

I load up my waterproof speaker and hold it above my head playing 'I Will Always Love You'.

He laughs and rushes downstairs, through the front door and out into the rain.

'I'm so sorry about the wedding, I was a jerk and shouldn't have let you go.'

His smile beams, but I think he could be crying. It's hard to tell in the rain.

'Will you go out with—'

He cuts me off with a deep and passionate kiss, I can't help but drop the speaker and pull him in close.

'You get her tiger.' The little old lady watching from next door calls out and we break apart and laugh.

I don't know what the future holds. All I know is right now, right here, I am finally happy. Still messy. But happy.

THIRTY-EIGHT DEGREES SOUTH

jodi cleghorn

Heidi stopped at the caravan door and contemplated the showering paraphernalia in her arms. Why bother? Solace wouldn't be found in a caravan park shower block, the first week in January, with a whinging five-year-old in tow. It had taken the first real sleep-in for six months to see the stupidity of forcing their home routine here. Besides, it was after 10 am. If they hurried, they might still beat JD and the girls to the beach.

Noah sat on the edge of the unmade bed, waiting for the inevitable hustle to his second-least-favourite part of the day. She dumped the toiletries bag and towels beside him.

'How about we skip a shower?'

'No shower.' Noah leapt up and broke into an impromptu victory dance. 'Woo hoo.'

'Reckon you could handle going straight to the beach?'

The exaggerated air punch and yesssssss made her laugh.

'How 'bout you get our swimmers off the line. I'll pack some lunch.'

He bounced down the caravan stairs, whistling. The semi-musical hiss stopped when he negotiated the plastic strips hanging in the door, moving from happy bard to stealth operative in a heartbeat.

Not for the first time, she wished she could be more like him, less like herself: go from one thing to another with little thought for what was left behind. Baggage came with responsibility. It came with being an adult. She struggled to balance responsibility with fun the way JD did. Meeting him had motivated her to be less uptight.

'Mu-um. JayDee's here.'

She smiled at the way Noah elongated the vowels in the abbreviation and grabbed her robe, tying it over her boxer shorts and singlet.

In the warm, muted annex light, JD looked as out of place as Noah did.

Over the years, the sun and salt had bleached the green and orange stripes to peach and spearmint. Despite renovating the van's interior—a brand-new kitchen, floor coverings, upholstery for the U-shaped dining area, and an upgraded inner spring mattress—her father had kept the canvas annex as a time capsule. She swore she could still smell Burger Rings, Le Tan sunscreen, green Impulse body spray, and Southern Comfort.

At the far end was the same set of bunks she and Harry had fought over, until their father had hammered out a time-share agreement of the top bunk to end the sibling squabbles. They'd spent endless rainy Easters on the floor playing Uno and Monopoly with their holiday mates. There'd been endless replays of *The Goonies* and *Top Secret*. In their final years at high school, the floor became a sprawling raft of teenagers sleeping off whatever booze they could get their hands on until they didn't want to go to Anglesea any more.

There'd been the Gold Coast. A trip to Bali. And a year in London where she'd met Elliott.

And now there was Noah. And JD. As incongruent as each other in the intersection of the present and past.

JD hung his sunglasses from the neck of his T-shirt, a smile on his tanned face, as he waited for his eyes to adjust. So at ease in the world. So different to Elliott.

'You left this last night.' He held up her cake plate. 'The girls ate the rest before we got up. Best breakfast ever, they said.'

Her face relaxed into a smile she was coming to associate with JD. 'Wish I could eat mud cake for breakfast.'

'Hey JayDee?' Noah's eyes were full of excitement, and Heidi didn't know if it was missing a shower or the unexpected appearance of JD. 'We're going to the beach *without a shower*.'

'You have a shower before going to the beach?'

'Not anymore,' Heidi said and reached down for the swimmers and towels in Noah's hands. 'Where are the girls?'

'My parents took them to Lorne for a picnic. I thought, perhaps I could take you and Noah out for brunch?'

'Brunch?'

She couldn't remember the last time anyone asked them out for a meal. Now two in the space of twenty-four hours.

'If you're busy—'

'No. No we're not busy. It's just—'

'Why don't I take Noah up to the bouncing cushion and let you have a shower in peace?'

Heidi laughed and ran a hand through her messy hair. 'You don't know just how good that sounds.'

'Maybe while you're gone, you'll think about coming to the surf club tonight? With me. They've got a live band.'

'Oh, I—'

'My folks offered to have Noah. The old man would love to have him over again. I'm a bit of a disappointment, you know, producing three daughters.'

'Can I Mum? Pah-lease. I wanna go.' His small body wiggled and he started to jump around. 'Pah-lease? Granddad Keith rocks.'

Heidi knotted her fingers together. 'I don't know if I can ask them to do that.'

'Please-please-please?'

'You didn't ask,' JD said. 'They offered.'

'But—'

'MUM?'

'Noah, please, just give me a moment.'

'Hey Junior, what do you think? Would you like to hang with Granddad Keith while I take your Mum out?'

'Sure. You should go Mum. Just no *kissing*.'

He screwed up his face. Heidi blushed and looked away.

'Only dancing.' JD held his hand up, thumb crossed over his little finger. 'Scouts honour, mate.'

Heidi caught the spark in JD's eyes though and her heart stuttered. 'Let's take it one deviation from the norm at a time.'

'Do you know my Mum does stad-istics.'

'In the department we joke they're sadistics.'

'Is there any way of strengthening the odds you'll say yes?'

Her blush deepened, pulling her into the past again; how Harry's summer best friend had courted her, if you could call it that, on the same steps.

'I think you've already done a good job of increasing your probability.'

Her smile was genuine. Easy. His in return coursed through her body like warm honey spiced with chilli.

Noah, tugged at JD's hand. 'Can we go bounce?'

The familiarity between them drew her in a different direction, stirring her guilt.

If you'd been a better wife, Noah would have this all the time.

If you'd tried harder, Elliott would still be …

'Heidi?'

'Huh, sorry. I …'

'An hour. And then brunch?'

What kind of wife —

'Yes,' she said, too emphatic for the conversation, barely defiant enough to silence the guilt. 'But in an hour it will be lunch.'

'And an hour closer to you saying yes to going dancing tonight.'

A cool, evening breeze blew across the river, tangling the hair Heidi had left loose around her face. She walked with JD past the surf shop, the general store, the Melaleuca Gallery and onto a new strip of holiday apartments.

'This used to be old Californian bungalows and vacant paddocks,' Heidi said. 'You ever get the feeling of dislocation ... when somewhere you used to know really well has changed when you go back? And you feel lost.'

'It felt like that when Ruth died,' JD said. 'That's why I sold the house. Everyone said I was crazy and I would regret it. But every time I walked into a room and she wasn't there, and I realised no matter how long I waited, she wasn't walking back in, I lost her all over again.'

Elliott had been everywhere too. A domestic suffocation where she struggled to draw enough breath to keep going; slow-drowning in his anger and despair. And when she left, she was grateful their new home had no trace of him. Just the moments he darkened the front door for his weekends with Noah. Ignoring his son, to hyperfocus on her, until he realised she wasn't coming back and he stopped taking his son for weekends.

And eventually Noah forgot.

Heidi pointed to the strip of fancy shops and more holiday apartments ahead at the bend in the Great Ocean Road.

'That used to be The Three Kings milk bar and takeaway. I remember being tiny and bouncing on the trampolines next to it. Twenty cents a go. There was a hardware store on the other side and now it's more holiday apartments.' Heidi sighed. 'I'm sorry. I talk too much. I'm kinda starved for uninterrupted adult conversation.'

JD took her hand and squeezed it. 'I know the feeling.'

Heidi waited for him to let go. His fingers snaked through hers, the sensation of being the smaller hand in the grasp foreign. But good. Right. He smiled at her and for the first time since Noah came along, she gave herself permission to fall into the moment and forget everything else.

She squeezed his hand back.

They walked on, in silence, to the bend, where music from the Surf Club filtered down from the dunes.

'You know what? I don't care if the band's shit and I don't know the songs,' Heidi said, her old spark igniting. 'For a few hours I just want to pretend this is all there is. Not that I wish ... oh shit. I mean, excuse my language. I—'

'It's okay, Heidi. I know what you mean. C'mon.'

The band worked its way through the usual '80s hits: 'Video Killed The Radio Star', 'Karma Chameleon', 'Billie Jean', 'Africa', and 'Take On Me'. Heidi grinned as she drank her beer, dancing on the spot until the opening bars of 'Footloose' spurred her into action. 'We're dancing. Let's go.'

She took the stubby from JD's hand and half-danced, half-dragged him onto the crowded dance floor. In the bouncing, sweating mass she lost herself, becoming one with the music. The thrill of JD's body shadowing hers, inching closer and closer.

When the crowd screamed the iconic 'cut footloose' refrain with the lead singer, JD grabbed her hand and spun her around and around. He dipped her backward at the end of the song, the two of them breathing hard when they came upright and face to face.

A pared back version of the Thompson Twins' 'Hold Me Now' washed across the crowd, shifting the tone.

JD slipped his arm around her, pulling her close to him. Heidi rested a hand on his broad shoulder and let him take her other hand in his. They moved slowly. The strict dancing position dissolved until Heidi had her head against his shoulder, eyes closed, awash in his comforting proximity. Her lips mimed the lyrics, body swaying with his.

If only she could stay here, with him, like this.

Thundering EDM replaced the final fading cord and the crowd dispersed. She imagined Australian backpackers dancing to the same song in London clubs and through endless nights on Ibiza. Six years ago she could name all the electronic dance songs. Now she had no idea.

JD relaxed his embrace, dropping his hand to her lower back to keep her close. 'Another beer?'

Heidi nodded. 'I've got to go to the loo. I'll meet you on the deck.'

A damp, red-faced reflection scrutinised her from the pitted mirror over the basins in the washrooms. Her guilt stirred.

What kind of mother leaves her son with strangers to go out dancing and drinking with a strange man?

She splashed water on her face, her foundation long gone, and scraped the damp hair back from her face.

What kind of wife chases —

'Fuck off,' she mouthed, glaring at her reflection.

The guilt, which always sounded too much like her ex-mother-in-law, shut up.

She forced a grin to her lips. A funhouse string of reflections winked at her. So many young Heidis from *before*. When she didn't know how far a human could break.

If only —

Heidi slammed the washroom door and strode into the crowd seeking what her guilt told her she could not have.

He sat by the deck railing, two stubbies on the table frosting with condensation. The ocean stretched indigo and glassy beyond the scrubby cliff top. Main beach, *their beach*, sprawled wide and empty at low tide. A roaring onshore break competed with the drum and bass, echoing her heart's driving rhythm. She exhaled the last of her inhibitions and dragged the chair opposite JD around to sit beside him.

'I haven't had this much fun in ... I don't know how long.'

She took a long drink from the stubby and considered how much honesty she dared.

That she found the way he parented as sexy as his arse in his fluoro green boardshorts. The way his waist narrowed and even though there was grey in his short hair, his stomach was as flat and arms nicely bulked as men twenty years his youth. The kind of buffed surfer she'd lusted after, without success, until she turned sixteen.

'I ... I've watched you ... how you ...'

Oh Heidi, c'mon. She coached herself. *Hold it together or he'll see straight through you, to what you really want.*

'... how you are both parent and friend to your girls. How you've got it all together ... and I realise I'm fucked up, but ...'

She put her hand up to stop him interrupting her.

Oh Christ, why did I have to point out I'm fucked up?

She took a steadying breath. 'JD, seeing you parent has given me hope and I thought I was all out of hope.'

'You're not fucked up, Heidi.' He slipped his fingers through hers, and stroked her palm with his thumb. 'You're beautiful and brave and Noah adores you. When I saw you on the beach that day, for the first time in years I felt ... something. Something I thought died with Ruth.' He leant closer. 'And every time I see you, every day we spend together, when we say goodbye I fear you'll walk away and I won't see you again.'

'I see you and it's like ...' She paused, her heart hammering. 'You're so full of life. I just want to—'

She kissed him before she lost her nerve. His lips yielded to hers. Electricity forked through her body, shocking her out of the long, numb sleep she stayed in to keep safe. His hand caressed the back of her neck. The beer on their tongues became a shared sweetness. His sandalwood aftershave mixed with the salty air and she wanted more than a kiss on the Surf Club deck. She wanted him naked and alone and all hers. His hands exploring her burning skin.

But as they pulled apart, the guilt tore free. A whiplash of turbulent emotions stole the oxygen, returning the suffocation she thought she'd escaped.

You should have loved him more. Like you loved, Noah.

Her seat pitched backward as she stood suddenly.

'I'm sorry. This was—'

She fled through the glass doors, back inside, unable to face the complexity of what she wanted. The human tide swallowed her. Hysterical laughter and leering faces zoomed in and out as she stumbled in different directions trying to find the exit.

You'll ruin him like you did Elliott.

Lost, riven by panic and guilt, she careened through the chaos. Trying to remember how to breathe.

'Heidi?' If she moved faster she could outrun him. She could outrun it all. If only her lungs would fill.

'Heidi!'

JD pulled her into his side and steered her out of the melee, into the foyer.

'What did I do wrong?'

'Nothing. It's me.'

'I don't understand.'

He tried to brush the hair off her face. She turned away from his touch and the reminder of what she couldn't have.

'Please talk to me.'

Heidi wasn't having that conversation here, where the guy manning the sign-in desk could hear. She shoved through the main doors and even though her pelvis told her running was for someone who hadn't pushed a baby through it, she sprinted down the hill, only stopping when she got to the road. JD caught her hand just as she went to cross.

'Heidi, talk to me. HEIDI?'

'I thought I could do this. I wanted it so badly, but I can't.'

'I'm sorry if I came on too fast.'

She stared at the initials drawn in the concrete, unable to meet his eyes.

'I need to get Noah.' She shook his hand free. 'Alone.'

'But—'

'You need to forget me, JD. Don't come to the van. Don't find us at the beach.'

'Heidi?' He ran across the road after her. 'Stop, please.'

'I lied to you JD,' she said, spinning around to face him. 'I'm still married.'

'But I thought—'

'I know. And I let you.'

Heidi dropped their bags beside the annex door and went back inside for her keys and the esky.

'Why do you need keys?' Noah asked.

'We're going to a different beach today. Point Roadknight. Awesome boats and rock pools. It's Grampy's favourite beach.'

'Will JayDee be there?'

She passed him the keys. 'How 'bout you pop the boot and put the bags in?'

'Sure, Mum.' The way his 'sure' mimicked JD's stabbed at her.

A minute later, Heidi heard voices near the car and went out.

Noah beamed. 'Look Mum, it's JayDee and Granddad Keith.'

'He's not your Granddad,' Heidi snapped, walking between Noah and JD, keeping her back to Noah and lowering her voice. 'I thought I made it clear I don't want you here.'

Noah looked up at her, confused. 'Mum?'

'C'mon sport. JD tells me you're pretty good on the bouncing cushion,' said Keith. 'Wanna show me?'

Noah looked between her and Keith, caught. She'd do anything to save Noah from a bitter scene, afraid of what he remembered from her and Elliott.

'Half an hour, okay?'

'Yessssssss.' Noah ran and jumped beside Keith's older, slower stride.

JD waited until they were out of earshot.

'Noah told the old man his dad was sad and got sick and had to go live somewhere else to get better.' His eyes held onto hers. 'Why didn't you tell me?'

Heidi swallowed hard, fighting to keep her composure.

There was no recrimination in JD's voice, but the idea of talking about her ex undid her. She'd already cried an ocean of tears for him, for Noah, for everything lost.

'Elliott is Noah's dad. We met eight years ago in London. He was funny and talented and had all this zest for life. And it wasn't so much that Noah was unplanned, more it was easier than we thought it would be. I have friends on their third and fourth rounds of IVF.'

Heidi leant against the car.

'They tell you having a child will expand your love. Will bring you closer together, but Elliott was ... jealous of Noah. He didn't like the way it changed us. Noah didn't sleep. I had to go back to work when he was six months old. I was tired all the time. I didn't have it in me to be what Elliott needed.'

Heidi shielded her eyes from the sun. Clouds gathered on the horizon, promising a cool change later.

'It would have been easier if he'd just hooked up with one of the girls at work to get his needs met. Instead, Elliott swung from crushing depressions into manic furies. I see all the warning signs of bipolar now, but back then I had a little boy who'd just started walking. Funding cuts were threatening my job. I was barely surviving.

'Then Elliott got sacked. It turned out his job was the only thing anchoring him and without it he became even more ... *unpredictable*. I tried. I did. But I had to keep Noah safe. I had no choice.'

JD's expression remained gentle, understanding, as she unpacked the betrayal she swore everyone could smell on her like shit.

'He came for Noah that morning and I wouldn't let him go. A year earlier, one of the guys he grew up with drove his car into the main irrigation channel and killed himself and his two kids.'

'I read about it,' JD said and rubbed his eyes. 'I didn't understand it then and I don't understand it now.'

'Elliott hated himself,' Heidi said. 'And he hated Noah.'

'And you, Heidi. You said you're still married.'

She reached out a toe to draw a line of dots in the dirt.

'It's a dog act to divorce your husband who's in full-time care because he didn't quite kill himself.' She scrubbed the dots out. 'My in-laws hate me. They blame me for what happened because it's easier to do that than accept their perfect son was flawed.'

'I'm so sorry, Heidi.'

200

'Not as sorry as I am.'

She walked back into the annex and sat in the caravan doorway, bare feet on the worn sea-grass matting.

Next year it would be gone. Her father had finally capitulated to building a permanent aluminium annex. Room for her and Noah, and the family Harry looked like he was keen on having now he was married. She admired her brother for still believing in love, despite all she'd gone through. In years to come, Noah would have cousins to play with. They'd fight over who slept on the top bunk. They'd out-cheat each other at Uno and binge watch their favourite movies.

'I like you, Heidi,' JD said. 'Being with you is like the sun coming out when you thought it was gone forever.'

There wasn't enough space in the caravan door to sit beside her. He knelt and took his hat off, running his hand through his short hair. The grey less obvious in the half-light.

'And I know there is more to what you're telling me than *what you're telling me.*'

He laid the cap and his sunglasses on the floor beside him.

'What do you want?' He rubbed at his stubbled chin. 'Not what's best for Noah. Or your ex. Or whoever you think has more say in your life than you have. What do *you* want?'

Heidi rested her head against the aluminium door frame.

'I don't know. For years I just wanted things to be better.'

She pushed her toes into the sea-grass matting's roughness.

'I don't know what you want, but I know you look happy— peaceful—on the beach. You come up grinning after you've dived under the waves. And on the dancefloor you look fierce and kind of wild. It's like you haven't a care in the world.'

'But I do. And that's the problem.'

JD touched the top of her big toe. Brushed the dirt off it.

'Everyone has a right to start again.'

Heidi thought of Elliott, confined to a bed in a nursing home. The mush he tolerated sometimes and the feeding tube when he couldn't. The adult nappies he lived in, when he had never once changed Noah. And how there was something of him still there, trapped inside a body he'd destroyed.

'Heidi, it's summer. Come back to the beach with us. Come over for BBQs. Let's go for bush walks. I won't ask you for anything. I don't expect anything. But if you want something more, I'd like that.'

He stood and pulled her to her feet.

'In a few weeks, when we go home, if that's it, that's okay."

Her hand felt small in his larger one again. An anchoring disparity. One she wanted to grab tight to. But ...

'I don't want to lead you on.'

'I choose you for now. What do you want though?'

'I just ...'

She looked to the plastic annex window, rolled up to let the air in. She'd once sat beneath it, while everyone else was out and done something she'd been waiting summers for. Had Harry's summer best friend kissed her? Or had she kissed him? All she remembered was she'd taken his hand, as she took JD's now, and pulled him down onto the sea-grass matting. It was the same fluttering tumble-turn in her stomach when she sat cross-legged, closed her eyes and gave herself over to summer's possibilities.

.

CONTRIBUTORS

Australian **ANNA CAMPBELL** has written 11
multi award-winning historical romances for
Avon HarperCollins and Hachette Grand Central
Publishing. As an independently published author,
she's released more than 35 bestselling stories.

Anna has won numerous awards for her Regency-set stories,
including *RT Book Reviews* Reviewers' Choice, the Booksellers'
Best, the Golden Quill (three times), the Heart of Excellence
(twice), The Write Touch, the Aspen Gold (twice), and the
Australian Romance Readers' favorite historical romance (five
times). Her historical romances have been translated into more
than 20 languages.

Right now, Anna is working on several connected series of
books all set amidst the glamour, elegance, and sensuality of
Regency Mayfair. In 2024, she plans to complete the *Scoundrels
of Mayfair* series with *The Last Duke She'd Marry* (February) and
The Duke Says I Do (June/July).

Anna enjoys working with aspiring writers to help them
achieve their dreams and has run numerous workshops across
Australia on writing romance and commercial fiction. She lives
near the river in Brisbane and loves to travel the world seeking
inspiration for her romantic stories.

You can find Anna at

annacampbell.com

206

A.K. LEIGH is an academic, identical triplet, hyperlexic (neurodivergent), writing workshop presenter, and author of over twenty romance genre fiction and non-fiction writing books.

She holds post-graduate qualifications in counselling, editing, and writing, all of which she draws upon in her writing. Her PhD research through CQUniversity has resulted in the conceptualisation of three theoretical models for application in literary theory and trauma theory. This research includes the identification and definition of the post-trauma romance subgenre, making A.K. the world's leading expert in the field.

Some of her passions, and areas of expertise, include trauma theory, romance writing, identical triplets, and neurodiversity. She also writes under the pseudonyms Alicia Leigh and Leigh Hatchmann.

You can find A.K. Leigh at

fallinlovewithleigh.com
amazon.com/author/akleigh

JAN-ANDREW HENDERSON is the author of 40 children's, teen, YA and adult fiction and non-fiction books. He has been published in the UK, USA, Australia, Canada and Europe by Oxford University Press, Collins Books, Hardcourt Press, Amberley Books, Oetinger Publishing, Mainstream Books, Black and White Publishers, Mlada Fontana, Black Hart, and Floris Books.

He has been shortlisted for fifteen literary awards in the UK and Australia and won the Doncaster Book Prize, The Aurealis Award and the Royal Mail Award—Britain's biggest children's book prize. He has appeared in many anthologies and had plays performed as far apart as Texas and the Edinburgh Festival.

He runs The Green Light Literary Breakdown Service (editing services), is a professional member of the Institute of Professional Editors and teaches online writing courses.

You can find Jan-Andrew at

janandrewhenderson.com

CHARMAINE CLANCY is an Australian author, presenter, and educator.

Her works include novels for kids and teens, although sometimes she writes short stories for grown-ups. She's even won awards for some of her stories.

Charmaine is passionate about helping students who have struggled with literacy and inspires them to create their own stories they can be proud of. As well as teaching at high school, Charmaine presents holiday writing workshops for children of all ages and hosts the annual Rainforest Writing Retreat.

All her books are written with humour and dogs. Life is better with both.

You can find Charmaine at

charmaineclancy.com
Facebook, Instagram or Twitter

CHRIS RADGE is an Australian novelist based in Brisbane, Queensland where she writes full time and is a part-time stay-at-home NanMa.

Her published works include Anthologies: 'Smithy' in *Short Stories of Mystery and Murder*, 'Tinsel Fructify' in *Short Stories of Forests and Fantasy*, 'Ghost Writer' in *Short Stories of Ghosts and Graves*, 'Frankenstein's Legacy' in *Short Stories of Science and Space*, 'Rounder' in *Meanwhile Murder*, 'Trigger' in *Got Game?* 'Brewing Love' in *Splashes of Love*, and 'Feathered Hooves' in *From the Edge, WAG*.

Published picture books include *Sneezes*, a rhyming book and *Yarn*, teaching to always look for the good in everything. *The Billabong Mermaid*, and *The Frog Hotel*, TBP 2024.

She is currently engaged in writing an octology of YA Urban Fantasy books called *The Elder Scale Series*.

She was a 2022 & 2023 judge for the Aurealis Awards, a member of Queensland Writers Centre, Romance Writers of Australia, Gold Coast Writers Association, Brisbane Writers Group, Writelinks, SCBWI, the Australian Fairy Tale Society, and looks forward to the Rainforest Writing Retreat every year.

As co-host of RWR and the editor/organiser/typesetter of this anthology, she always enjoys the journey from beginning to end.

You can find Chris at

chrisradge.com
christinetitheradge.com

LIZZ CURRY is a local Gold Coaster who has never learnt to surf. She is currently working on her first novel, and when not writing, she is looking after her two energetic children or teaching high school music.

She received fourth place in the Gold Coast Writers' Association short story competition in 2023. She has since made plans to enter more competitions so as to have more to say about herself.

You can find Lizz at

Facebook: lizzcurryauthor

KELLIE M COX draws on her clinical experience to create complex and engaging characters. Published with Strong Female Protagonists her book titles include, *Murderous Intent, The List, The Reef, Advice for Life,* and *The Last First Kiss.*

Her stories traverse the globe, taking readers to cities they dream to visit from Paris, Rome, Berlin, Bora Bora, and the Mekong Delta. Her own travel stories forming much of the inspiration for the settings and colourful characters readers fall in love with.

Kellie connects with her writing tribe through GCWA, QWC, ASA, Rainforest Writers Retreat, Helensvale Writers Group, Sisters in Crime, Somerset Storyfest, and Fiona McIntosh's Masterclass graduate group.

When not writing or seeing clients in private practice, she can be found on the beaches of the Gold Coast flooding her social media with photos of her gorgeous dogs.

You can find Kellie at

kelliemcox.com

CHRISTINE BETTS writes novels about women, love and Paris, short stories about sisters, Bali and lost girls, and blogs about creativity, travel, and the inner life. A firm believer that writers will save the world, she writes daily and passionately encourages everyone around her to join in.

She is obsessed with Paris but lives on Bundjalung country with her family and cats.

'Death of a Show Princess', Shortlisted for the Scarlet Stiletto Awards (HC)

'Tough Crowd', Winner, QWC Nov 2021

'How I Got this Tattoo', Winner, The Tasmanian Writers Prize for 2022

'Southbank', Shortlisted, BWF First Date at Southbank

'Undetected', co-authored with Kate Kelsen in *Meanwhile Murder*

'A Tale of Twin Towns', Published in, *Tales from the Pandemic: an anthology.*

'Fancy Meeting You Here', Honorable Mention, QWC Aug 2022

'Delete World', co-authored with Kate Kelsen in *Got Game?*

Awarded the 2023 Gold Coast Writers' Association Andrew McDermott Annual Achievement Award

You can find Christine at

writerpainter.com

In 2020, **SELENA JANE** published her debut
fiction novel, *Search for the Holy Whale*, a coming-
of-age story about our connection to animals and
Mother Earth.

Nominated for the BX Business awards in
2021 & 2022 for her content and copywriting business, Selena
helps business owners share their passion project with the world
through creative content.

Serving as the Website Content Manager for the Gold Coast
Writers' Association from 2020 to 2023, she currently holds the
position of Publicity Coordinator and has been on the panel of
judges for the association's short story competition for the past
two years.

Her short story titled, Angle Wings are Precious Things, *Got
Game?* anthology 2023.

A mother, business owner, world traveller, animal lover,
marathon runner and avid reader, Selena appreciates a well-
written book, with great characters and a good story line.

You can find Selena at

www.selenajane.com

214

DEBBIE KAHL has dreamt of writing fiction since she was a teenager obsessed with the *Sweet Dreams* books that cluttered her bookshelf. Despite an on-going battle with author imposter syndrome, Debbie has continued to write contemporary fiction for tweens, teens and adults winning the inaugural Book Links QLD Mentorship and the CYA Conference Unpublished Chapter Book for middle grade readers, along the way.

When she's not writing, you can find Debbie teaching English and Japanese at a high school in Brisbane, where she finds lots of inspirations for her stories. Debbie is also an integral part of the CYA Conference team, which aims to provide professional development opportunities for young adult and children's writers in Australia.

You can find Debbie at

debbiekahl.wordpress.com
LinkedIn

ANGELA VICTOR is a Brisbane-based author with a weakness for brooding heroes, witty dialogue and good coffee. She works for a university and, in her spare time, writes Regency romance and dreams of her next travel adventure.

Angela's husband and son are great supporters of her writing, unlike her cat, who hinders every step of the process. One more jog along the keyboard may see Smokey traded in for a well-behaved goldfish ...

Angela is currently working on the next book in her steamy Regency series.

JARED KRANZ likes to write ... music. But as he lives on a small house block and has to 'keep down that damn racket' he had to find other hobbies that didn't result in weekly visits from noise abatement officers.

After reading one too many books where he was forced to skim pages due to uninterest he had that same thought which naively crosses most early author's minds, that of, 'I could write that.' But no. No he couldn't. At least not at first. But as failing is what he does best, Jared set out on a long line of authorial quests to hone his skills and fail and fail again until he got it right. He may still claim to not have it 'right' but it's a darn sight better than where it was. But then maybe, you can be the judge of that.

MARTIN CLANCY, an avid storyteller with a passion for all forms of stories. Currently, she's honing her craft further through a scriptwriting course, and eager to explore new avenues of storytelling.

As a proud member of the trans community, she infuses her work with themes of inclusivity, diversity, and acceptance. She strives to evoke emotions, provoke thoughts, and transport readers to realms where anything is possible.

In every story she tells, she aims to champion the importance of representation, ensuring that every reader sees themselves reflected in the pages of her work. Her love for storytelling knows no bounds, and she's dedicated to creating narratives that embrace and celebrate the diversity of being human.

JODI CLEGHORN's word witching adventures traverse fiction, poetry, tarot and depth work. Her novellas *Elyora* and *The Starling Requiem* were Aurealis short-listed in 2012 (horror) and 2018 (science fiction). She is the co-author of the  epistolary novel *Postmarked Piper's Reach* with Adam Byatt. *This Once Precious Life* is her legacy short story collection.

As the co-owner and publishing editor of eMergent Publishing, Jodi birthed six conceptual short story anthologies and gave dozens of local and international authors their debut publication. In 2011, she was the publishing oomph behind the charity anthology *100 Stories for Queensland* and the recipient of the Kris Hembury Encouragement Award.

Jodi's penchant for the dark vein of humanity has swung from speculative fiction to post-trauma romance. This is her first publication in her newly-adopted genre.

You can find Jodi at

subscribepage.com/jodicleghorn

REVIEWS

Your words are as important to an author as an author's words are to you.

GOODREADS.COM

Please leave a review

AMAZON.COM.AU

Feed an author, leave a review. It takes five minutes and helps more than you can imagine.

ACKNOWLEDGEMENTS

RWR would like to thank Chris Radge (Christine Titheradge), Charmaine Clancy, Gina Pinto, for their hard work in assembling this anthology.

Likewise, thanks are also due to the RWR retreaters/authors, without their work there wouldn't be an anthology.

Big thanks to all the crew at the Self-Publishing Lab for everything you do. You can contact them at selfpublishinglab. com for a website setup and publishing needs.

And the biggest thanks to Charmaine who thought that a writing retreat would be a great idea and has run with it ever since.

SPLASHES OF LOVE

 ## Online **Classroom**

The Lab is packed with in-depth, step-by-step practical video lessons, tools and resources on preparing, producing, publishing and promoting your book. PLUS the 24/7 community and coaching you need to ensure you achieve your full potential and goals.

 ## Book **Creation**

Let us take care of these one-off tasks, so you can avoid any headaches. Our team is ready when you are. The Lab is an award-winning one-stop shop for creating and publishing a quality book with a team of professionals who care. Oh, and you'll have fun doing it too!

 ## Book **Marketing & Coaching**

From Amazon Ads, building email lists to selling at tradeshows, the Lab has you covered. With courses, templates and our online community, all your questions can be answered with the support of the Lab team and other like-minded authors achieving their goals, just like you.

About the **Self-publishing Lab**

The Lab is an award-winning publishing destination helping thousands of writers avoid the traps in publishing and get started on the right foot.

With over 25 years in the publishing industry, Anthony and the team at the Self-publishing Lab continue to help authors become bestsellers, sell thousands of dollars worth of books online, at schools, workshops and to organisations.

Here's what makes the **Self-publishing Lab different**

 No contracts or exclusive agreements that sell your soul. You'll keep 100% royalties and control without it costing you an arm and a leg to publish your book.

 We show you how to use technology to sell more books while you sleep, even if you're a tech newbie.

 Have your book distributed and available for purchase online around the world, at bookstores and libraries in print and e-book.

Contact Us Today

 w: selfpublishinglab.com
e: support@selfpublishinglab.com

 PO BOX 187
Browns Plains, QLD
Australia, 4118

Rainforest
Writing
▼ Retreat

WANT TO WRITE A NOVEL?
DON'T KNOW WHERE TO START?

Join us at Australia's favourite writing retreat.

LEARN

Immersive workshops, mentoring & publishing tips from International best-selling authors and industry experts.

CONNECT

Find the support you need and new life-long friends who share your passion. Network, laugh and connect.

PUBLISH

Every year, RWR puts out a high-quality anthology only open to Retreaters for submissions.

SECURE YOUR SPOT!

Each year, sixty writers gather at the spectacular Australian rainforest. Many of our writers have gone ahead to publish their first works because of the ongoing support and guidance they receive. RWR can book out over six months ahead, so get in early and secure your place. Once you have become a Retreater, you'll also be invited to our private mastermind group, meet-ups, extra workshops and qualify to submit to our publications.

www.RainforestWritingRetreat.com